NO NAMES. NO PROFESSIONS. NO SMALL TALK. PERFECT ANONYMITY.

NO STRINGS
attached

JIFFY KATE

More Books by Jiffy Kate

Finding Focus Series
Finding Focus
Chasing Castles
Fighting Fire
Taming Trouble

French Quarter Collection
Turn of Fate
Blue Bayou
Come Again
Neutral Grounds
Good Times (coming summer 2020)

Table 10 Novella Series
Table 10 part 1
Table 10 part 2
Table 10 part 3

New Orleans Revelers
The Rookie and The Rockstar
TVATV (coming fall 2020)

Smartypants Romance
Stud Muffin (Donner Bakery, book 2)
Beef Cake (Donner Bakery, book 4)

Standalones
Watch and See

One

THE LIGHTS FLICKER, ALERTING EVERYONE THE PROGRAM IS ABOUT TO begin. I place my empty glass on the bar and turn to the attractive blonde waiting for me.

"Are you ready?" she asks politely, slipping her hand into the crook of my elbow.

"As ready as I'll ever be." Letting out a soft laugh that does nothing to quell the nerves beginning to build in my stomach, she leads me down a dark hallway.

When we reach our destination, she gives my arm a reassuring squeeze and turns on her six-inch heels, leaving me with a small group of men. We look like a bunch of cookie-cutter assholes—expensive suits, clean-cut faces, two-hundred-dollar haircuts.

Chuckling to myself, I release a breath and with it some of the pressure building in my chest.

It's like when I'm a few hundred feet from a summit or on a downhill slope of an off-road ride. My body needs to pressurize, or my chest will explode from the adrenaline spiking.

An older woman steps out from behind a curtain and explains the rules of the game, but she gets drowned out by the blood pumping forcefully through my body. It's okay. I know what I signed up for.

My name is called and my body tenses. A blindfold covers my eyes, and my remaining senses are called to action. The mixture of smoke and perfume in the air assaults my nose while the taste of the whiskey still lingers on my tongue.

My skin tingles with excitement as my ears focus on the voices calling out from the crowd.

I'm led onto the stage and introduced. Cheers and whistles greet me, boosting my confidence and allowing it to overshadow my fears. My guide, Cindy, loops her arm through mine and turns me in a circle, pausing briefly so the audience can get a good look at my ass.

Once I'm turned back around, Cindy instructs me to remove my jacket, which I'm happy to do. The stage lights are fucking hot. As sounds of appreciation begin to die down, she then asks me to remove my shirt.

Even though this is my first time being an active participant, I've been here before as a spectator, and I know the fun is just about to begin.

It's amazing how the loss of my sight makes it so I can *feel* everyone looking at me, watching me. It's thrilling, liberating, and my pulse speeds up in anticipation of what's next.

There's a hum—an energy—that takes over the room.

Now that the crowd is primed and ready, Cindy interrupts the low roar. "Let's start the bidding at fifty dollars."

Bids start flying, but I don't pay attention to the numbers being shouted. However, there seems to be a bidding war going on and it fuels my eagerness.

My dick begins to stir.

As a victor is announced, everything begins to feel like an assault on my senses—women yelling, hot lights, anticipation. I'm caught off guard when Cindy places my hand into the hand of the winner.

Warm, soft skin somehow puts me at ease. Her palm isn't sweating, but I bet mine is. She seems to be the opposite of me in every way I can judge—smaller, calmer, confident. I gladly let the woman lead me down the front steps of the stage and maneuver me through the crowd, away from the noise.

When she stops abruptly, pushing me forcefully against a wall, my dick immediately stands to attention, remembering why we're here.

"I can't wait to get my hands and mouth on you," she growls softly, her lips brushing my ear, making me ache for her touch. Pulling on my hand, she practically drags me down what I'm guessing is a hallway.

Close by, behind closed doors, the muffled sounds of other people fucking fill the air.

As much as I love the visuals of sex, *hearing* people scream out in pleasure is simply intoxicating. The sounds caused by an orgasm are almost as good as the feel of one.

We turn a corner and the woman holding my hand stops, opening a door and leading me through. Once the door is closed behind us, she sighs. The relief in her voice matches exactly how I feel.

I want her.

I have no idea what she looks like or what her name is, but she's all I want.

Her hands on my face are the only warning I get before her mouth attacks mine. Soft, sweet kisses don't exist here, only raw and passionate, needy and devouring. Her fingers brush over my erection through my pants, and I hiss at the contact, causing her to groan.

Before I can recover from the heady kiss, she has my belt undone and my pants on the floor, guiding me backward. Pushing on my shoulders, she forces me down until I'm sitting, and then her touch is gone. The sound of two heavy shoes hitting the floor is followed by the rustle of fabric, and my pulse quickens with the thought of her being naked. Listening to her undress is the sweetest torture, and I briefly worry I won't last long when I'm finally buried inside her.

Quick, loud breaths fill the room—hers and mine.

She doesn't sound nervous, just turned the fuck on, which makes me even harder, if that's possible. Her sweet, musky smell teases the air, making my mouth water. Sensing she's close, I reach out. The tips of my fingers graze skin, and latch on, beginning to explore. I'm rewarded with toned legs. Working my way up to her hips, I squeeze her flesh, relishing how soft and full she is, before pulling her to me. My mouth connects with her smooth stomach, and I kiss it, my tongue tracing the area around her belly button, nipping at her flesh.

She runs her fingers through my hair, scratching my scalp, and I practically purr. I don't think I can wait any longer.

I need inside her.

I need release.

Sliding my hand farther down, I find her bare pussy and slip my middle finger through her folds to see if she's ready for me.

"Fuck."

I can't help but sink my finger as deep as it'll go, my palm putting pressure on her clit. Her soft gasp fills the room. Adding another finger, I pump into her, twisting as I pull out. When I bring them to my mouth, tasting her, she groans, her hands tightening in my hair.

She likes my fingers.

And she likes me tasting her.

"You taste so good," I tell her, unable to hide the smirk on my face, loving that her breathing has picked up and she has me in a vice grip.

She's turned on.

She wants me.

And she tastes like good and evil all wrapped into one.

I want to taste more of her, have her mouth on me, but I can't wait any longer.

I have to fuck her.

Now.

As if she read my mind, she releases me and I hear the rustle of a foil packet. She rubs her hand up and down my shaft a few times before sliding a condom into place. I smile when her hands go to my shoulders and she straddles me, loving that she's just as impatient as I am. When I lean forward, my mouth finds a nipple, and I greedily suck it into my mouth, swirling circles around the peak with my tongue. Her breasts are full and heavy in my hands, and I'm hopeful I'll get the opportunity to fuck them, too.

She whimpers, her hips rising, impatiently searching for friction.

Releasing her tits, I grab my dick and drag it through her wetness, eliciting more whimpers and groans, pleas for more.

"Take it," I tell her. "Take my cock."

Bracing herself on my shoulders, she slides down, making us both moan in pleasure.

So. Fucking. Good.

"Yes," she breathes out.

Giving her a moment to adjust to my girth, my mouth goes back to worshipping her luscious tits.

She's an altar and I never want to leave.

Slowly, she begins to move and my hands find her hips, gripping them as

I move her up and down my dick.

"Oh, *fuck*," she moans, and I couldn't agree more. I keep my lips latched onto her tits, carefully biting her nipple every time I thrust into her. She pushes my shoulders until I'm lying down flat, but she stays sitting up in order to ride my cock.

I love the blindfold, but I wish I could watch her. She moves with wild abandon under my hands, and the smack I give her ass only encourages her, making her yelp and then moan, "Oh, God."

I'm not God, but right now, I feel like one.

She gets louder and louder as I feel her pussy start to tighten and spasm around me. I find her clit with my thumb, and she screams as her orgasm takes over her body in waves. It seems like there's more than one. I allow her to squeeze and ride it out until I can't take it any longer. The sensations are too much for me to handle, and I flip her onto her back so I can speed up my thrusts.

Grabbing for her leg, I hold it up by my shoulder, angling myself to go deep, wanting to feel her come again. I press into her clit.

"You...feel so damn good. So warm...so tight," I tell her, my words and breaths coming out in pants as I feel my balls begin to tighten. Chills cover my skin and I fucking come like I've never come before. The spasms are so forceful I can hardly hold myself up. I'm still recovering, groaning at the sensation of her hips slowly meeting mine, when she reaches up and removes my blindfold.

We share a brief moment of eye contact, and I'm not surprised at all that she's the most beautiful woman I've ever seen. And it's not just the lack of blood in my brain.

She's fucking gorgeous.

I'm not sure how long we stare into each other's eyes, but it crosses a line of comfort...longer than necessary, longer than what is acceptable for someone you just met...fucked.

Suddenly, her soft, warm body tenses and she begins to move, working her way out from under me.

"Thanks," she says, standing and immediately going for her clothes lying over the chair in the corner of the room.

I watch as she slips a white lacy dress over her head, only given the pleasure of her backside. Her wavy brown hair is messy and falls loosely around her shoulders.

Between the mind-blowing orgasm and the vision of her, she has me entranced. It's not until she starts to put her foot into a black combat boot that I realize she's going to leave, causing my heart to leap into my throat.

I'm still lying here with my cock out. She can't just leave.

"Where are you going?" I ask, my voice sounding a bit panicked.

She looks up at me halfway through pulling her second boot on and just stares at me. Then she squints her eyes before furrowing her brows. "I'm leaving." Her tone is clipped, and she sounds annoyed, nothing like the breathy, panting moans from ten minutes ago.

"Yeah," I say, sliding off the bed. "I see that." I pull my pants back on, tucking my dick in safely before zipping up. "But I don't even know your name."

Standing there, she gawks at me like I have a third head, but she doesn't say anything, just continues putting herself back together. Her fingers comb through her hair, trying to tame it. She has the freshly-fucked look perfected, and I smirk again, knowing I did that to her.

When she turns toward the door, I feel the need to fill the silence, say something, anything to make her stay.

"That..." I say, pointing back to the bed. "That was phenomenal." I sound like a lawyer arguing his case, daring her to disagree with me.

She turns around and sighs deeply, crossing her arms over her chest. "It was pretty good." The quirk of her eyebrow and twist of her lips makes me want to press her up against the wall and show her *pretty good*.

It was fucking at its finest, and she knows it.

"Pretty good?" I question, my voice getting louder.

"Look," she says in exasperation, "I've gotta go." She doesn't give me another second, not even a backward glance. She just picks up her bag off the floor, tosses it onto her shoulder, and walks out, leaving me there with a semi hard-on, half-dressed.

She still turns me the fuck on, even though she's blowing me off.

"Thanks!" I yell out the door behind her. I want to run after her, but she's apparently done here. *We're* apparently done here. Looking around the room, I check to make sure I didn't leave anything. When I see the blindfold on the crumpled bed, I walk over and lean across to grab it. Unable to help myself, I breathe deeply, desperate for any lingering proof that the sex was as good as I thought it was. That happened. The sheets smell like sex—like her and me. I think about stripping them off and taking them too, but instead, I shove the blindfold in my pocket and walk out.

I know it's supposed to be fucking without any connection, like a one-night stand on steroids. And I was okay with that, in theory. I thought I could do it—get an adrenaline rush all while getting my dick wet. Get in and get out—no strings attached. But now, I'm not so sure.

That might have been the single most amazing sexual experience of my life, and I don't even know the girl's name.

I'm obviously going to have to do this again.

It can't end like this, with her walking out on me and never seeing her again. I need to at least know her name and maybe what her plans are for the next fifty years. At the very least, I need to fuck her one more time.

Two

"So," Sebastian says, making himself comfortable, perched on the edge of my desk. "How did it go?"

"It went," I tell him, staring at my computer monitor, suddenly feeling close-mouthed about the whole thing.

He scoffs. "Yeah, dipshit. I was there." Pausing, I know he's waiting for me to expound on the situation. When I don't, he huffs out his frustration as he stands and places both hands on my desk, leveling me with his stare. "I want details."

"She was...great." I almost said *pretty good*, but I don't.

"Just *great?*" he asks, making it sound like an insult.

I let out a deep breath through my nose and run a hand through my hair. "It was phenomenal. The best fuck of my life. Is that what you want to hear?"

His face splits into a wide, knowing grin as he nods his head. "*That's* what I'm talkin' about." He claps his hands together and walks over to the pool table that sits in the middle of my office. "You wanna head back over there with me again this week?"

Racking the balls, he waits for my reply, but honestly, I don't know. Sure, it was pure ecstasy, but what if I don't get so lucky next time? What if the next time is horrible? I could get a wanna-be porn star and have to listen to twenty minutes of exaggerated moans of pleasure. Or she could be a squealer. I've never liked that.

What I really want is to know *her* name.

I want to be with *her* again.

I don't want another random fuck.

Sebastian breaking the balls brings me out of my thoughts. "I don't know. I might be busy this week."

"What's with you, Jude?" He pockets a stripe and continues around the table, looking for his next move. "You've been acting weird since last week. I thought maybe it was because you didn't like it, but you say it was phenomenal, so what gives?"

"That's the thing. It was *so* phenomenal I don't want to try it again."

He's going in for another shot when he suddenly stops, his eyes still on the green felt of the pool table. "So, you're saying...What *are* you saying?" he asks, looking up at me with a confused expression, similar to the one *she* gave me.

"I'm saying *she* was phenomenal."

"Oh, shit. You didn't get all weird on her, did you?" he asks, worry etching his face. "Look, man. I got you into the club on my word. You mess this up and I'll beat the shit out of you. Do you know how hard it is to even get an invite?" His face is turning red as his eyes squint in accusation.

I got the rundown before I ever stepped through the doors.

After handing over a clean bill of health, there are no questions asked.

Everyone is anonymous.

No names.

No professions.

No small talk.

Perfect anonymity.

That's what draws people there: one hundred percent no strings attached.

I thought it wasn't going to be a problem.

But that was before I saw her.

"What happened?" Sebastian asks, balancing his stick against the pool table.

I sigh, leaning back in my chair. "Nothing. I didn't do anything, but I thought maybe we'd hang out for a while...have another round," I admit, but just hearing those words come out of my mouth makes me realize where I went wrong.

I got attached.

In those thirty minutes of bliss, I allowed her to do more than fuck me. She got under my skin. When our eyes met after she took my blindfold off, something passed between us. I felt it and I know she did too. There's no way she didn't. The connection was palpable, like another entity in the small room.

And I want more.

"But I didn't do anything," I assure him. "I wanted to, but I didn't. She said she had to leave, and she did. That's it."

"You know if you see her again, you can't act like you have some claim on her. There's no caveman bullshit at the club. It's her prerogative, man, just like it's yours. That's the beauty of it. No strings attached—"

Gritting my teeth to hold back the growl of frustration I feel ripping its way up my throat, I interrupt him. "Yeah, I got it. I know all of that."

"So, you wanna go give it another shot? Maybe you need to fuck her out of your system?" he offers.

"I don't know if I can."

As he goes back to knocking balls into pockets, he asks, "She was that good, huh?"

"Fuck, yeah," I say, the wistfulness in my voice betraying me, exposing all the things I'm not saying. Shaking my head, I try to clear the thoughts of her as they flash through my mind. The way she felt in my hands. The way I fit inside her. Her smell. Her taste. Those deep chocolate eyes. That wild brown hair. The contrast between the lacy dress and those fucking combat boots.

I want her.

She intrigues me.

I want to know more about her.

Sebastian walks over, scrubbing his hands over his face. "Listen, dude. Sometimes you hook up with someone who completely rocks your world. It doesn't happen to everyone, and it rarely happens more than once. Someone like her is an enigma. She got under your skin. I get it. But you've gotta drop it. Let it go."

Pinching my bottom lip between my fingers, I turn my attention to the window. "Yeah," I say in agreement, but I don't mean it. I don't want to do any of that. I kind of hate that she got under my skin, but now that she's there, I want to keep her there. Maybe I will go back to the club. Maybe she'll be there. Maybe I can talk to her. "I'll go back with you this week."

"There ya go," Sebastian says, slapping me on my back. "Hop back in that saddle and ride 'em." Winking, he grins as he pretends to gallop around my office.

He's so fucking ridiculous, but I can't help laughing at his antics.

"I'm not getting back on the block again, though. Not this week. I think I'll just sit back and observe, have a few drinks."

Sebastian shrugs, picking his pool stick back up. "Whatever you think, but I'm tellin' you, another woman, a different pussy...that's what you need. It's just what the doctor ordered."

"I'll think about it."

"So, did you think about it?" Sebastian asks loudly over the music playing. The lights are down, and bodies grind against each other on the dance floor. This is the pre-party to the big show. A little warm-up, if you will.

"I'm just gonna hang back for tonight," I tell him, letting my eyes roam over the people, searching for her.

Sebastian eyes me with a knowing look. "Don't do anything stupid. Remember what I said."

"No strings attached," I say, nodding my head. "I get it. Don't worry."

I really don't have any plans of doing anything to compromise the agreement. I just want to see her, and I need a few drinks. It's been a crazy week at the office.

The advertising industry can be stressful sometimes, or maybe Sebastian and I just make it that way. Everything in our office always turns into a competition, and we've had season tickets for the Texas Oilers on the line the last few months.

Mr. Stephens promised them to us if we steal the McDavid account out from under our competition. I really want those tickets. They're supposed to have a good season next year. I also want to show the losers at Friedman and Associates who's boss.

So Sebastian and I have been going above and beyond to land this account. We've even slept a few nights at the office this past week. We both deserve a night to blow off some steam.

I must say, I'm a little jealous that Sebastian will be getting pussy tonight, and there's a good chance I won't.

Maybe I should reconsider and go on the block.

Sure, I could go to a normal club and pick up a girl, but then I'd have to call her and take her out on a date. The reason I agreed to come here with Sebastian in the first place, besides his incessant begging, was because I just needed to get laid. I thought I was looking for what this place offered. I didn't expect to get this worked up over a one-night stand.

When did I grow a vagina?

I take a deep breath, slapping my hand down on the bar. Sebastian's right. I need to fuck her right out of my head. Turning to find Cindy and ask her to put me on the list, I see *her*.

She's traded the white lace dress for a red one. It dips down between her tits, almost to that smooth stomach I explored with my tongue. Her hair is pulled up off her shoulders, exposing her long, slender neck.

My mouth begins to water as my dick stiffens in my pants.

I watch her mingle with the crowd. A guy walks up to her and offers her a drink, but she declines. She lingers by the side of the stage, but she doesn't interact much. When the lights flicker to let everyone know the bidding is getting ready to begin, I make my way around the back of the room, squeezing between people until I'm standing right behind her.

I'm so close I can smell the same subtle, sweet smell I've dreamed about since last week. It's intoxicating. I want to run my nose up her neck and inhale her until I've had my fill, and then I'd like to taste her again.

But first, I need to talk to her.

I glance around to see who's watching, but I know Sebastian is getting ready to go up on stage, so I don't know what I'm worried about. No one else here cares who I'm talking to, but my stomach feels nervous.

She must sense someone standing close behind her, because before I have a chance to lean in and say anything, she turns around. When recognition hits her, she squints her eyes and furrows her brows as her jaw tightens. "Hey," she says, looking me up and down.

"Hey," I say with a dip of my head and a slight smile, hoping to ease any reservations she might have. It usually works like a charm.

Turning back around, she takes a small step closer to the stage, away from me, which in turn makes me take a step closer to her. I just want to be near her.

"So," I say quietly, leaning in closer. "I meant to ask you the other night what your name is."

"I wouldn't have given it to you." She looks over her shoulder. "It's not part of the deal."

I mean to laugh quietly, but it comes out much louder. This woman is so damn sexy. And the fact that she plays hard to get makes me want her even more. "I know it's not part of the deal, but I just figured that since we—"

"Let me guess," she interrupts, whipping around to face me. "You figured that since we fucked, you deserved to know my name?" Her eyebrow raises and she purses her lips. "Well, here's the deal. *I* bid on you. It's what *I* wanted. So *you* don't get to *figure* anything. Now, leave me alone."

A lady's voice comes through the speaker we're standing next to as she introduces the first person up for bid. When a hand goes up in front of my face and I realize *she's* bidding on him, my heart begins to pound in my chest. Someone else raises their hand, upping the bid, and I begin watching every hand that goes up, hoping they'll outbid her.

When a busty blonde ends up winning the war, I let out a sigh of relief.

As the second guy comes up on stage, she bids again. It ends up being a battle between her and a woman on the other side of the room. I see her glance across at the woman and then back up at the guy on stage. I don't know what comes over me, but when she lifts her hand to bid again, I reach up and pull her arm down. The woman down at the other end wins the bid, and the one in front of me is now shooting daggers with her eyes.

"What the *fuck* is your problem?" she spits out, a little louder than I would like. A couple of people standing nearby look over at us. She grabs my arm, and I immediately give in to her, loving how my body feels when she touches me.

Forcefully, she pulls me to the back of the room before she spins around and faces me. Her eyes are full of fire as she squares her shoulders. "You don't get it, do you?" she asks with a wicked smile on her face.

"I just...I didn't want you bidding on that guy," I tell her, stumbling over my words, trying to make my actions seem like they make sense. "You can have me for free. You don't even have to bid."

"Oh, my God." She rolls her eyes and glances up at the ceiling, as if she's trying to rein in her fury. "Listen," she says, putting her hand on my chest and pushing me back. "This is obviously not the scene for you. Leave before I have Kirk escort you out," she demands as she motions to the guy standing by the door with arms as big as tree trunks.

When I see that she's serious, and not wanting the wrath of Sebastian if I were to get kicked out of the club, I slowly step back and nod my head in acquiescence. Turning, I walk out the doors.

It kills me to walk away from her, knowing she's probably going to end up bidding on some lucky motherfucker and he's going to get a taste of heaven— *my* taste of heaven.

I leave wanting her more than I did last week, and that's saying a lot.

Three

"WHAT THE FUCK, DUDE?" SEBASTIAN ASKS AS HE HANGS FROM MY door frame. His scrunched forehead and eyebrows tell me I have disappointed the beast.

"I got cold feet."

Lie.

"Bullshit."

"There weren't any women there that looked attractive, so I bailed."

Lie.

"Bullshit."

"Fine," I groan. "I just wasn't into it. Once I got there, everything felt wrong. I didn't feel like going through with it." Frustrated, I abruptly stand up and let my chair roll into the wall behind me.

"So, let me get this straight. All you had to do was put on a blindfold, walk up on stage, and get laid. How could you not *feel* like it? You're speaking some broke-ass language. It doesn't compute." He folds his arms over his chest and stands there, waiting for more of an explanation.

Sometimes, Sebastian acts like a fucking girl, always wanting details and shit. And talk about micromanaging. Holy fuck. This dude is the king. "She was there, wasn't she?" he asks, quirking an eyebrow. "She was there, and you got spooked. Please tell me you didn't try to talk to her again."

I stand there, facing off with him, trying to think of something to say to get him off my dick.

"Holy shit," he says, taking my non-response as a response. "You did, didn't you?" He begins to pace the floor in front of my desk. "Did they kick you out? Did *she* have you kicked out?"

"No." I roll my eyes, thinking back to our confrontation and how fucking sexy she looked when she was pissed off.

"Okay, okay. That's good. What did she say?"

"Nothing."

Lie.

"Really? She didn't say anything at all?"

"She asked me to leave," I say quietly, staring out the window of my office. I'm not ready for his psycho bullshit. It's just a fucking club. He acts like he's going to get excommunicated from pussy or something.

He scrubs his face, squeezing his eyes shut. "Maybe you're not cut out for this after all."

"That's what she said," I admit, sitting back down in my chair and leaning my head against the wall. "I still can't believe she told me to leave. I thought maybe once she saw I was just a regular guy that she might want to talk to me, maybe have a drink...go on a regular date."

"Some girls don't want regular," he says, leaning over my desk. "She's there for a reason. You should've stuck to the rules. Who knows? You might've gotten lucky, and she might've bid on you again."

Would she? Just thinking about it makes my heart beat faster and my dick stir in my pants. Maybe I should give it one more shot, go up on stage, give her a chance to bid on me again.

"I know what you're thinking," Sebastian says, backing away from my desk. "But I think you should probably give it a few weeks before you go back. If she said anything to Kirk, he might have you on the blacklist. Let the dust settle, and then you can give it another shot."

Nodding my head in agreement, I let out a frustrated sigh. I need a few weeks anyway. I need to figure out if I even want to go back. Plus, I'm too buried in work to be buried in pussy. I need to keep my head on straight and land this McDavid account. And snag those Oilers tickets.

I can smell the peanuts and Cracker Jack from here.

Sebastian is standing beside me with a smug, satisfied look on his face.

"You went to the club last night, didn't you?" I ask as we strap on harnesses to climb the big-ass wall in front of us.

We have a lot of things in common. We both love the challenge of working in the competitive world of advertising. We're also adrenaline junkies and we'll do just about anything once.

Our weekend adventures typically require some sort of safety gear—bungee jumping, skydiving, mountain biking, rock climbing—and includes anything that gets our blood pumping.

It's why I decided to give the club a try. I'm always up for a new adventure.

"Yep," Sebastian says, eyes straight ahead.

"How was it?" I ask. What I really want to know is if she was there. It's been over a week since she told me to leave. I decided it was best to give the whole club scene a break. But I've thought about her every day since, hoping I might run into her somewhere...anywhere—gas station, grocery store, walking down the street. The fact we live in a big city and I'd never seen her before that night doesn't bode well for another chance encounter, though.

Sebastian sighs and shakes his head. "Dude, I think I owe you an apology." The serious look on his face when he finally turns to look at me makes my stomach drop a little, and not in a good way. Not like when I'm jumping off a hundred-foot bridge.

"Why?" I ask in a hard tone. I stop adjusting the harness I'm wearing and start climbing up the wall, needing a distraction.

Sebastian stays silent for a minute. I look back, and he's still standing on the ground, fiddling with his rope.

What the fuck?

"Sebastian?" He looks up at me and starts to climb, quickly reaching where I'm hanging on to the wall.

His face is sheepish and whatever the fuck he needs to tell me, he better say it quick before I punch him for no good reason. It must be bad for him to have so much trouble spitting it out.

"I—I was with this girl at the club the other night," he begins, and it makes me feel sick to my stomach. "She was..." He sighs, shaking his head. "Fuck, Jude. She was everything. And when I left, I started thinking about what you were saying and how you felt. I thought you just weren't cut out for the club, but then I met her, and she fucked my whole world up."

"What did she look like?" I growl, stalled out on the wall. Thankfully, there's no one coming up behind us and no one close by, because I swear if he starts describing *her*—my girl—I'll kill him, right here, hanging from these damn ropes.

Realization flashes across Sebastian's face and he pales. "Jude, dude. I'd never."

I know that. I know he'd never intentionally fuck a girl I was into. I know him better than that. But what if he fucked a girl I was into and didn't know it?

"Just tell me what she looks like." The red-hot anger bubbling up inside me is unfamiliar. I'm not usually hot-tempered, but something about the idea of Sebastian, or any other fucker, being anywhere near her pisses me the hell off.

He hesitates for a second and then says, "She, uh, had these amazing blue eyes...like the bluest eyes I've ever seen."

I let out an audible sigh of relief and shake my head. Did I really just get that worked up over someone whose name I don't even know? *What the fuck is wrong with me?*

"And she's so fucking tall," Sebastian continues. "Like, almost as tall as me, without heels," he says in awe.

"It's not her." I close my eyes and take a deep breath, refocusing my energy back to the wall.

"Thank fuck." He throws his head back and hangs off the wall, letting the harness support him. When he looks back up, he starts climbing and I follow in step. "So, tell me about her. I need to be prepared, just in case."

I laugh, but there's little humor behind it. This whole thing is so messed up. Why couldn't she just tell me her name and let me take her out on a date?

"She's shorter, kinda petite, but the way she can level you with her stare makes her seem taller, you know? And she smells fucking amazing...like sugar with a hint of spice. She's got this wild brown hair that matches her eyes, and both times I've seen her she was wearing these beat-up combat boots." I say the last part and smirk. "She's unlike anyone I've ever met before." That's all I'm willing to say to him about her right now. Normally, I'd go on about a girl's tits or the way she felt when I was inside her. Sebastian and I are worse than a bunch of gossiping girls. We usually tell each other all kinds of shit, but not this time.

"So, what are you gonna do about it?" he asks.

"Honestly, I have no idea." I think on it for a second and wonder briefly if it's all about the chase. Maybe I want this girl so damn bad because I can't have her? "I think when shit settles down, I'll go back to the club and hook up with someone else, fuck her out of my system. I don't have time for dates and shit anyway."

"Yeah. Sure," Sebastian says. "That usually works." He doesn't sound very convincing.

Normally, Sebastian is all for the no-strings-attached, no-questions-asked rules of the club. He firmly believes that life is just one big fuck fest. But something seems different with him. His tone makes me think he's second-guessing his ways.

"What about you?" I ask, working up a sweat as I pull my body up to the next rock that's jutting out.

"I don't know, man."

"Did you try to talk to her?" I ask, knowing this change in attitude has to be about the woman he fucked.

"I tried to abide by the rules, and I tried to stay cool, but fuck if watching her walk out wasn't the hardest thing I've had to do. Actually, fuck that," he says, grunting as he pulls his mammoth body up higher. "I went back the next night, trying to get a glimpse of her," he admits, focused on the top of the wall we're approaching.

I smirk, because I love the tables have been turned on his ass. Now he knows how it feels.

"I just went to have a few drinks and hang out. I didn't even think she was there until I saw her walk past me with a guy in tow. I almost tackled the guy and carried her out of there over my shoulder, but somehow, I managed to stay glued to the barstool. She never even looked my way." His voice sounds pained, and I feel for him. I don't know what I would've done if I'd had to witness that. I'd probably have lost my shit.

"Fuck, Bash. That sucks." I climb up one more rock, wondering how we went from two carefree dudes to schmucks who cry over girls. "You know what? Fuck 'em. We don't need that shit."

"Yeah," Sebastian grunts.

"So are you going back next week?"

"I don't know," he says as we reach the top. "Maybe you're right. Maybe we should fuck them out of our heads."

I nod in agreement as we rappel back down the wall, but I have my doubts that going back to the club is the cure for what ails us. Somehow, a woman I know very little about has become all I think about. I'm not sure fucking someone else will get her out of my head. I'm not sure I could even get my dick up for someone else right now.

Normally, after exerting so much energy, I feel better, but as my feet hit the floor, I feel more worked up than I did when I got here.

Four

It's been three weeks since I've been to the club, but Sebastian thinks it's safe to come back. So, tonight's the night, under strict orders to not talk to her if I see her.

I agreed to it, but only to pacify Sebastian. I can't make any promises. I just need to see her and find out if she still has the same effect on me.

When I walk into the club, the buzz I felt the first night I came here is thick in the air. The lights are low. The music is pumping through the speakers. There are women dressed to kill and drinks flowing freely. Sebastian and I pre-gamed before coming tonight, hoping to loosen ourselves up enough to get a grip and get back up on that stage.

It's the first step in Operation: Fuck the Women Out of Our Heads.

The lack of creativity in that shows exactly how screwed we are.

"Let's do this," Sebastian says as he tosses back another shot of 1800. I do the same and nod my head. I'm to the point where I don't even need a chaser, which means I should be able to do this without reservation, but she's still there in the back of my mind. I've let my eyes roam the room, searching her out, but that mess of brown hair is nowhere to be found.

Sebastian slaps my shoulder and then grabs on to my suit coat, pulling me toward the hallway where we line up to go on stage. We've already put our names down for the night.

"Good to see you boys back," Cindy says, winking as she walks down the line, checking off her list. "Are we ready?"

Most of the guys are loud in their approval, but I notice Sebastian doesn't say much. Neither do I. He turns around and gives me a pointed look before slipping his blindfold down over his eyes and allowing Cindy to walk him out on stage.

The crowd cheers as she introduces him and starts the bidding process.

My stomach is in my throat. I shouldn't be nervous. It should be easier this time.

I continue to listen to the bidding as it goes higher and higher. Finally, a winner is announced and I'm a second from bolting back down the hallway when Cindy pops her head around the curtain and tells me I'm up. Turning to look at the exit, I think about it, but then say fuck it and slip the blindfold over my eyes, allowing her to lead me blindly onto the stage.

Even though my eyes are covered, I can still feel the heat from the bright lights, and a few beads of sweat pop up on my forehead.

"Let's start the bidding at fifty dollars," Cindy announces. This feels like the first time, but deep down, I know it's not going to be anything like it. I had hoped that she might be here and bid on me, but I didn't see her. Hell, she probably wouldn't bid on me even if she were here. She was so pissed the last time I saw her, demanding for me to leave. Thinking of that night and the fire in her eyes causes my dick to twitch. I'm completely unaware of my surroundings, lost in my nerves and thoughts of her when Cindy announces a winner.

I swallow thickly as a hand grips my arm. The woman leading me doesn't say anything as we walk, people brushing against me as we make our way through the crowd. Part of me thinks I would know if it was her if I could just hear her voice...or smell her. I can't get those things out of my mind. They're what I think about on a daily basis when I'm jacking off in the shower.

A door opens, and I'm pulled inside. The hand that was touching my arm begins to push my jacket off my shoulders, and I allow it. She pushes me back until my knees hit the bed, and I sit, reaching out to feel her.

The second her lips are on mine, I know they're all wrong. My hands move up her legs to her hips, and they're all wrong too. They're too bony, not enough curves. Her smell is flowery, like roses, not the sweet and spicy I was hoping for. My breathing increases, and she takes it as a sign of arousal, but I'm slowly starting to freak the fuck out.

I don't want to do this.

This is all wrong.

She's all wrong.

She makes quick work of the buttons on my shirt but leaves it on and moves down to the button of my slacks, sliding the zipper down and going straight for my cock, which is confused as shit. It's semi-hard due to the touch and excitement, but not as hard as it would be if it were *her*.

Her mouth assaults mine again, and I don't return the kiss.

"What's the matter, baby?" she asks, her voice too high-pitched, too nice. "Are you nervous? Lay back and let me make you feel good."

I do as she tells me, but the second her mouth touches my cock, I push her off. "I can't," I say, ripping the blindfold off. When my eyes adjust, I see the startled look in the blue eyes looking back at me. She's attractive. Her blonde hair is long and straight. She'd be a girl I would've hit on or been happy to take home a couple of months ago, but not now.

"I'm sorry," I tell her. "I just...this isn't my scene." I repeat the words that were said to me a few weeks ago, realizing they're true.

She covers her bare breasts and her expression changes from startled to mad...or hurt. "Just go." She looks away toward the door, and I take the opportunity to zip my pants back up and grab my jacket.

"Sorry," I tell her once more before leaving the room. I know this is probably the last time I'll be able to come here. There's no way they'll let me in after this. The only thing that pisses me off about that is I'll probably never see *her* again, but that's probably for the best.

I've gotta move the fuck on.

When I'm finally outside and the night air hits me, I take a deep breath and rake my hand through my hair, trying to get a grip. I rode with Sebastian, so I walk to his Hummer and lean against the side of it, taking a minute to wrap my mind around what just happened.

I watch as a few people straggle in and out of the club. From the outside, it looks like a warehouse. There are no signs, nothing signifying what goes on inside those walls. It's part of the attraction. It's exclusive, elusive. Tons of people want to get on the list. It took Sebastian months to get me in, and now I've fucked it all up. It's not like I was serious about it. It was just another adventure, something new to try.

I never expected to meet someone who would fuck my head up so bad.

"I didn't think I'd see you back here."

The familiar voice makes the little hairs on the back of my neck stand up and my head jerks toward the sound of gravel crunching. *It's her.* She's standing about ten feet away, not nearly close enough, and wearing a tight black dress and those fucking combat boots. Her hair is pulled up on one side, but it's still messy. She has a backpack tossed over her shoulder. It's kind of weird. Most girls carry purses, not big, bulky backpacks.

"I, uh..." I stumble over my words, not knowing what to say. "Yeah, well, here I am."

It's dark, but we're standing close to a street light and it allows me to see a small smile on her lips. "Did you get what you came for?" she asks suggestively, nodding to the club entrance.

Her boldness and the fact she's not demanding me to leave shocks me. "No," I say, laughing harshly under my breath.

She tilts her head like she's trying to figure me out. "Well, I've gotta go," she says, looking down at the phone in her hand. "I'm running late."

"Okay," I say, nodding like an idiot, trying desperately to think of something intelligent to say but coming up blank. She makes me stupid. "Do you need a ride?"

"No." She smirks and starts walking away. "But thanks," she says over her shoulder. Before I can say anything else, she's gone. She slips into a beat-up Volkswagen and cranks it up. The dress, the boots, the ride...Everything about her makes me want to know more.

As she's driving off and I'm watching her taillights, I think of a million questions I should've asked her.

What's your name?

Wanna go out sometime?

Can I call you?

But it's too late, because she's gone.

The fact she was there and was probably with some other man makes my fists clench. My jaw tightens as I try to get my temper in check, because right now, I want to walk back in there and beat the shit out of every guy who might've slept with her.

Why does she come here?

Where is she going?

So many questions and I probably won't ever be able to ask them. I won't be able to come back here anymore. Besides the fact that they probably wouldn't let me in, I don't think I can come here and see her and know she's been or will be with someone else. It'll kill me, or I'll kill them.

"I wondered where you took off to," Sebastian says, walking up to his truck. "I thought you'd be at the bar." He unlocks the doors, and I get in without saying anything. His voice sounds almost as wrecked as I feel. We both sit in silence as he pulls out of the parking lot.

"That was fucked up," Sebastian finally says, leaning back in his seat as he drives us away from the club.

"Tell me about it," I mutter, rubbing my temples to try to rid my brain of the clusterfuck I've managed to get myself into.

"I took the blindfold off when we got to the room," he says quietly. "I just had to know."

"So, did you fuck her?" I ask, wondering if that's what I should've done. Maybe it would've done the trick. Maybe the blonde would've rocked my world, and I wouldn't be sitting here wondering how I can track down a gorgeous brunette when the only thing I know about her is that she's beautiful and she drives a fucking Volkswagen.

"Yeah, but I wasn't into it. She was taller, but her hair was jet black. She was decent. It was just..." He stops, running a hand through his hair and exhaling a deep breath. "I don't know, man."

"Wrong?" I ask.

"Yeah, *she* was just all wrong."

"I know the feeling." I'm weirdly relieved that he went through with it and is still messed up. The last thing I need is regret over fucking the wrong girl.

"What happened with you?"

"I bailed."

"Shit."

Sighing, I lean further back into the seat. "Yeah, probably won't be on the list anymore."

"Probably for the best."

As I watch the city pass by, I wonder where she was going. What was she late getting to? Or who? "I guess so," I say, resting my elbow on the door. "But

I saw her."

Sebastian's head whips my way. "Really? Before we went on stage?"

"No, after. Just a few minutes before you walked out."

Thinking back to seeing her standing there, looking like a fucking dark angel in her black dress and combat boots, I shift in my seat.

"Did you get her name?"

"No," I tell him, getting more frustrated with myself for not getting my head out of my ass. "She said she was running late, and then she was gone."

"Well shit, man. Now what the fuck are you gonna do?"

"I'm going to forget about her, and I won't be going back to the club."

Lie.

I might not go back to the club, but there is no way in hell I can forget about her.

Five

"Damn, you need to get laid," Sebastian says, breathing heavily as he rides up beside me and stops. Taking his helmet off, he pulls out his water bottle from his backpack and wipes the sweat off his forehead. "I'm all for extreme sports, but you're about to kill me out here today."

"I just need a good burn to help clear my head." I wipe the sweat off my brow and squirt some water in my mouth and then on my hair before restrapping my helmet. "Come on," I tell him as I begin to ride up the hill. "Let's hit a couple more trails before dark."

On our way back down the last trail, I feel my back tire cut loose. In the dim light, I can't tell where I'm going, but the next thing I know, me and my bike are barreling down a hill—separately. A rock gouges my leg and then my back. Something sharp hits the corner of my head, and then—

"Jude!" Sebastian yells. I must've blacked out for a minute. His voice is up above me, but it's loud and alarmed. "Jude, damn it. Answer me!"

"Shut the fuck up," I groan, rolling over and feeling a searing pain in my leg.

"You scared the shit out of me," he says, sliding down the hill and stopping himself right above me. "Are you hurt?"

"My leg hurts like a son of a bitch."

As Sebastian leans over to examine it, I can't help but reach down and feel around. My shorts are torn, and there's blood, but the sting in my leg keeps me from touching any more.

"That's gonna need stitches," he confirms, using the light on his helmet to get a better look. "We've gotta get you to the hospital."

"I don't know if I can walk back up the fucking hill."

"Well, then, I guess I'll carry your ass."

"Fuck no!" Bracing myself on the ground and holding my injured leg up, I try to stand. Sebastian's arms wrap around my waist, and he hoists me the rest of the way, letting me support my weight on him. Somehow, the two of us manage to climb back up the hill.

"You just had to do another trail," Sebastian says as we reach the top, both of us kneeling on the ground to catch our breath.

"Shut up."

"I'm gonna help you the rest of the way down the hill to the Hummer, and I'll come back for the bikes."

"Mine's probably beat to shit."

"I'm sure it's salvageable."

Half an hour later, Sebastian makes it back to the truck with the bikes and loads them up. My leg is throbbing so bad I can feel my heart beating in it. Before he'd gone back for the bikes, Sebastian tied an old t-shirt around the cut to keep blood from getting everywhere.

"What hospital?" he asks, driving back out to the main road.

"Whatever's closest."

He hauls ass and gets us to Mercy Hospital around ten. It's late, but the emergency room is packed. It must be a full moon or some shit, because there are crying babies everywhere and a pregnant lady making laps. There's also a dude over in the corner with a broken nose and a busted lip and what looks like a split above each eye.

"Wonder what the other guy looks like?" I smirk, pointing over to him.

"No shit. Dude got his ass handed to him."

"Harris," a nurse in blue scrubs finally calls from the ER entrance. Sebastian helps me up and lets me lean on him as we make our way back. The nurse points to a bed and pulls the drape closed, informing us a nurse will be with us shortly.

I've only been in an emergency room twice before—once when I was younger and had poison ivy so bad my eyes were swollen shut, and the other time when I passed out and broke my nose. My mom insisted on me being checked out, even though there isn't shit they can do about a broken nose. But I'm surprised I haven't ended up in the ER more than that. As much as Sebastian and I push the limits with our extracurricular activities, you'd think we'd be frequent fliers.

"I fucking hate hospitals," Sebastian says, grimacing. "The smell makes me feel sick."

"I was just thinking that I'm surprised we haven't ended up here before now."

"No shit," he says, laughing. "Remember that one time we went skydiving and my chute didn't open all the way?"

"Yeah, you were spinning like a fucking top. I just knew I was going to be scraping your ass off the ground."

"Nope," Sebastian says, shaking his head and puffing his chest out proudly. "I tucked and rolled that bitch. Didn't even walk away with so much as a scratch."

"You're the luckiest bastard I know."

We're still laughing when the curtain pulls back, and my heart tries to pound out of my chest.

What the fuck is she doing here?

Her eyes flicker—a moment's hesitation. She almost walks out, but then she doesn't. She puts both hands on her hips and looks over at me with a pointed stare. "This better be legit."

"What the fuck?" Sebastian asks, looking at her and then back at me. We're both staring each other down, but for different reasons. My heart is beating fast, and I can't keep my cock in check. She's standing there in scrubs with her brown hair twisted up in a messy bun. She looks different. There's no sexy dress, no combat boots. Her face is the same, though, intense eyes and pouty pink lips. The glare I've become accustomed to is also firmly in place.

"Look," Sebastian says, standing up. "You need to fix his leg so we can get the hell outta here."

Her eyes leave my face and go to my leg. When she sees I really am injured, her expression changes, and she goes into action. "What happened?" she asks, genuine concern in her tone as she peels the soiled t-shirt away from my leg.

I look down at the name tag that's hanging precariously close to her fantastic tits. *Roland, Quinn.* I can't help but smile. Knowing her name feels like

Christmas. And she's a fucking nurse. My shitty luck just got better. I almost forget about the huge gash on my leg because being in the same room as her and knowing her name is enough of a distraction to take away the pain.

She's turning my brain to mush.

"So, what happened?" she asks again, looking back up at me when I fail to answer her. "To your leg…"

"Oh, uh…we were mountain biking, and I lost control of my bike," I tell her, trying to keep myself from becoming the bumbling idiot she tends to turn me into.

"He did a fucking header down the side of a hill. I'm surprised he didn't injure more than his leg," Sebastian adds.

Coming closer, she pulls a light from her pocket and shines it in my eyes. "Any dizziness or blurry vision?"

"No," I say, swallowing hard when her hand brushes my forehead in an examining gesture.

"Do you need something for the pain?" she asks as she steps back and does a further assessment of my body.

Instead of answering with my words, I merely shake my head because everything going through my mind is completely inappropriate, and I don't want her to kick me out of her ER.

"Okay, hold tight. I'll be right back."

"What the *fuck* was that?" Sebastian asks after she's gone.

Unable to take my eyes off the curtain she just disappeared behind, I mutter, "That's *her.*"

"Her who?" he asks in confusion, until realization dawns. "Wait. You mean *her* her?"

"Yep."

"Well, *fuck me.*"

We sit in silence for a long stretch until Sebastian pats my good leg. "I'd stick around but I think you're in good hands." Then he makes a statement about being *parched*—his word, not mine—and scurries off to get something to drink. But I know what he's really doing. He's avoiding being around if and when I get stitches. He's not a fan of blood. He won't even watch *The Walking Dead.*

Fucking pussy.

"Still hanging in there?" she asks, peeking her head around the curtain. Shit, even her voice is sexy.

I want to hear her say my name.

"Yeah," I say, clearing my throat and readjusting myself the best I can. She wheels a cart in beside the bed with several sterile-looking supplies. The syringe is the first thing that catches my attention. Just seeing the long needle lying there makes me feel queasy.

Maybe I'm the fucking pussy.

With an air of pure professionalism, she goes to work, rolling up my shorts to get a better look at the wound. When her hand brushes close to my cock, it stirs against my leg.

He remembers too.

How good her hands felt.

How good she felt.

"I'm going to clean the wound first," she says, all business-like. "It'll probably sting a little." The coldness hits first and then the burn. And it more than stings. It hurts like a motherfucker, but I hold still, not wanting to show weakness in front of this woman. She's already made me weak enough by existing. If I go adding in wincing and crying due to a little cut, I might as well hand over my man card.

To keep from thinking about it too much, I stare at her profile. Her skin looks so soft. I want to reach out and stroke her cheek, tuck the few strands of hair that have fallen out of her bun behind her ear.

"So, mountain biking, huh?" she asks, keeping her head down as she focuses on her task.

"Yeah. I like extreme sports," I tell her, wanting nothing more than to keep her talking.

The corner of her mouth rises. "Really? Are you an adrenaline junkie?" she asks, picking her head up to look at me. Our eyes meet, and I know she feels this thing between us. I can see it in the way her gaze lingers and then her breathing picks up. She's trying hard to not feel it, but something deep inside tells me she does.

"I'll try anything once," I admit.

Eyes still locked with mine, she asks, "What other things have you done?"

"Bungee jumping, rock climbing, skydiving...If it's dangerous, I've tried it at least once," I tell her, refusing to be the one to look away. "What about you? Any hobbies?"

She cocks an eyebrow. "I have a few."

"Like what?" I ask, wanting to know everything about her, *knowing* there is more to her than a beautiful woman who frequents a sex club.

She shakes her head and goes back to work on my leg. "This'll burn," she says as a warning before sticking me with the needle. I'm so into her that it hardly fazes me.

As she waits for the numbing to take effect, I watch her.

And when she begins to sew my leg up, I still refuse to take my eyes off her.

When she's finished with the stitches, she wraps fresh gauze around my leg and begins tidying up the cart she wheeled in, preparing to depart. I try to speak, to say something, anything to keep her here. But then she's gone.

Always leaving before I'm ready for her to go. Always leaving me wanting more.

I lie back on the hospital bed and groan in frustration. She infuriates me and intrigues me and turns me the fuck on. I want her to want me like I want her, and I think she might, but she's not letting herself. There's something there. She refuses to acknowledge it, but I'm not going to give up. I know I said I'd forget about her, but fate just dropped her back in my lap, and I'm not letting her go.

Six

"Hey, Fergie. Wanna go to the park?" I ask, waiting for my blonde-haired beauty at the door.

She slides on the hardwood floor around the corner and gallops toward me, stopping just short of plowing into me. I think she wants to go to the park. I know I do. I need some fresh air and a quiet moment to think. We don't usually go on Sundays, but my leg is still healing, which means mountain biking is out, as well as bungee jumping and skydiving. I tried rock climbing the other day and wished I hadn't. So, the park it is.

I called Sebastian earlier to see if he wanted to meet up with us or grab some lunch later, but he sounded preoccupied and made up some lame-dick excuse of needing to run errands. Whatever the hell that means. He's probably out having the time of his life but doesn't want to tell me.

"We're gonna have our own fun. Aren't we, girl? We don't need big stinky Sebastian to have a good time." My girl wags her tail and looks up at me with her big brown eyes in anticipation. She loves riding in the car, even though it's a bit small for a dog her size. It's her head out the window that she loves the most, so the size of the vehicle has no bearing on her enjoyment.

When I bought the car, I didn't own a dog and swore I never would, but that was until this girl showed up on my doorstep. She was so little back then. I had no idea I'd be housing a small horse one day, but dogs grow up fast. By the time she was knocking shit off tables and taking over my apartment, I was already in love. There's no way I could give her up now. She's who I come home to at night and who snuggles up with me while I sleep. We share a jar of peanut butter and weeknight runs. Outside of Sebastian, she's my closest friend and the only girl I've wanted to have around past a few nights.

Girlfriends have just never been my thing. Up until a couple of months ago, I didn't want the attachment, but then Quinn Roland flipped my world upside down. Now, I don't know if I need to wind my ass or scratch my watch. She has me so worked up, and the fact that she still won't give me the time of day pisses me the hell off.

Now that I know where she works, I've been back once. I walked in with confidence, straight up to the nurses' station in the emergency room. Quinn didn't come see me, but she sent a message with another nurse, telling me not to come to her place of work again.

It wasn't my finest moment.

Cruising down the street, I look over and smile at Fergie, who has her big head stuck out the window and her tongue flapping in the wind. Glancing back at the road, I reach over and scratch her neck right behind her collar, just like she likes.

When we pull up to the park, I hook Fergie's leash onto her collar, and she follows me out of the car. After we make it safely into the gated area, I release her, and she takes off.

Picture the chick from *The Sound of Music* running the hillside singing, except make her a dog and turn the singing into barking, and that's Fergie right now.

I find a free bench where I can keep an eye on her, stretch my bum leg out in front of me, and watch her run and play with a few other dogs. It must feel great to finally be able to cut loose after being cooped up in an apartment all week. I mean, I take her out for bathroom breaks and walks, but she doesn't get to do this every day.

Maybe I should look into buying a house with a yard.

That thought catches me off guard. *Who the fuck am I?*

A few years ago, if you'd have asked me if I'd ever have a house with a yard, I would've said fuck no, because that's for pussy-whipped dudes who are attached to a ball and chain. Houses with yards are not for single guys like me who enjoy playing the field and living life on the edge. Sure, I'm not the most extreme dude around, and I don't get nearly as much action as a lot of guys.

Sebastian. But I live my life the way I want, no strings attached.

I have no reason to not want the bonds of matrimony and all that bullshit. My parents have been happily married for thirty-five years. My sister is also happily hitched. I just prefer to not be. I like adventure. I like trying new things. I like variety. I like space.

I also like Quinn Roland.

Why the fuck she just entered my mind while thinking about love and marriage, I have no idea. She's somehow worked her way into every facet of my mind without even trying. Usually, women are the clingers. They're the ones hanging around, wanting more. The fact that I can't get her out of my thoughts is troubling. I've tried everything. I've tried getting laid but couldn't go through with it. I've tried drinking her away, but it only made me want her more. That night, I tried to talk Sebastian into driving me to the hospital and pretending like I was sick. He wouldn't. Thank fuck. That might warrant a restraining order. I'm really not this messed up...or I wasn't, until her.

I let out a deep breath and try to think of something besides Quinn. I came out here to clear my head, but I'm not doing a very good job of that.

Scanning the large field for Fergie, I see her sniffing what I hope is just a patch of grass, when a little boy walks up to her and squats down beside her. I sit up a little, ready to go intercept if things get sketchy.

She's been great with the few kids she's been in contact with, but I don't know what this little dude's agenda is. He looks like he's talking to her and she begins to wag her tail, so I let them be for a few minutes.

The kid starts scratching behind Fergie's ears, and she licks him in the face. I wonder if he knows he's just made a friend for life. Her obsessive licking makes the kid fall on his back, but I can hear his laughter from here, so I know he's okay. Just in case, I decide to go over and check on him anyway.

Walking over, I call out, "Fergie." That gets her attention and she stops licking the poor kid. When I get to them, I look down and see a mess of brown hair and two large brown eyes squinting up at me.

He's a really cute kid. "Hey, buddy. You okay?" I ask, bending over to get a closer look.

"Yeah, she was just licking me."

"I saw that. She really likes for people to scratch behind her ears. She was just showing her appreciation."

"Yeah, I like her."

The kid can't be more than five or six. There are freckles splattered across his nose, and he has a big dimple in one of his cheeks. I glance around to see if an adult is looking for him because he seems too young to be unattended. That's when I see her—wild brown hair and a frantic look on her face. "Henry!" she yells, shielding her eyes from the sun.

I look back down at the kid and offer him my hand to help him up. "Are you Henry?"

He nods and smiles as he pets Fergie again.

I smile back at him because it seems as if the universe is on my side for a second time today. "He's over here," I call out, and the look on her face when recognition hits is priceless. She's in limbo between pissed and relieved.

"Hey," she says tersely, but her arms wrap protectively around the kid.

"Hey," I reply, watching them intently.

"Hey, buddy." She kneels down in front of him and holds his hands in hers. "You can't run away like that. Remember we talked about how if you can't see me, then I can't see you, and that's not okay?"

He nods his head, and his hair falls into his eyes. "Sorry." The tone in his voice is remorseful. "I just wanted to pet her," he says, pointing to Fergie, who is sitting on her hind legs, panting as she watches the three of us.

"She seems like a very nice dog," Quinn says, looking down at Fergie and then back up at me.

I nod my head and smile. "She is."

"Can I play with her?" Henry asks, pleading with his big brown eyes. I have no idea how anyone says no to that. I look back up at Quinn to see what she's going to do, and I can tell she's battling with what he wants versus what she wants.

"For five minutes," she tells him, and he and Fergie are off like rockets. I toss the ball over to him and tell him to play fetch with her.

"What are you doing here?" she asks, crossing her arms over her chest.

I laugh at her absurd question. "This is still a free country, and this happens to be our regular hang-out." I motion across the large green field.

"I've never seen you here before."

"Well, I've never seen you here before either." *Because if I had, I'd be here every day in hopes of seeing you.*

"We come here every Sunday," she says, watching Henry and Fergie play, and I add that to my *Important Things to Know About Quinn Roland* file. So far, it consists of: beautiful, guarded, drives a beat-up Volkswagen, wears combat boots, and goes to the dog park on Sundays.

"We usually come on Saturdays," I confess. She stands there, not offering up any more conversation, so I take it upon myself to do so. "Usually, Sebastian and I ride our bikes on Sundays or go skydiving or some shit like that, but I can't with my leg all fucked up. So, here we are."

"Language."

"What?"

"Watch your language." I look over at her, and she still has her eyes trained on Henry and Fergie, watching them like a hawk, or maybe she's just avoiding me.

"He can't hear me all the way over there."

She huffs, and I can't see her eyes, but I can imagine she just rolled them at me. "So you didn't follow me here?" she asks, her tone still a bit abrasive.

"No." I laugh again, because it sounds ridiculous, but when I think about my behavior over the past month, I can see where she might think I'd stoop that low. "Listen, I'm sorry for showing up at the hospital. I really just wanted to see you, and I thought if I approached you somewhere besides the club, you might agree to see me."

Her head whips around, and her brown eyes bore into me. "Don't bring *that* up in front of him either."

"Does he have some sort of special power I don't know about?" I ask, quirking my eyebrow. Sure, he's not too far from us, but he's completely preoccupied with my dog right now, and I doubt he can hear anything we're saying.

A small smile breaks across her face, and I feel myself relax a little. "No," she says, shaking her head and looking down at her feet. "Sorry, just a little paranoid about that stuff, I guess."

I smile, because this more vulnerable Quinn is different from anything I've seen from her before, and I like it. "Your secret is safe with me."

"She really does seem like a great dog."

"She is, and she loves kids."

"Do you have kids?" she asks, her voice softening.

I laugh again. "Uh, no."

"Henry loves dogs," she says.

"Do you have kids?" I ask, afraid to assume anything when it comes to her. She could be the big sister or babysitter.

"You're looking at him."

"Right, of course." I can see a stark resemblance—same messy brown hair, same big brown eyes. "He's yours." It's not a question or a judgment, just a realization. Things about Quinn start to make more sense—the wall she has up, her defensiveness.

"He is."

"He seems like a really great kid."

She smiles and nods, watching him and still refusing to make eye contact with me. "We've gotta go," she says, calling Henry back over. "Tell Jude thank you for letting you play with his dog."

"Thanks, Jude," Henry says, smiling up at me.

I'm smiling back at them, but inside, I'm a mess, wanting so badly to ask her to stay or if I can see her again...*when* I can see her again. But something tells me I shouldn't. Something tells me I need to play this cool and hope things will work out if they're meant to.

The universe has been good to me so far. I'll just have to trust in that.

"Maybe we'll see you again," I tell Henry, ruffling his hair. "Tell him bye, Fergie." On cue, Fergie licks the side of his face, and he laughs a big belly laugh.

Quinn does too and squints her eyes when she looks up at me. "See ya."

"Yeah." I nod and watch them walk away. When she glances back over her shoulder, my heart flips in my chest.

Seven

"The club. Tonight," Sebastian says as he walks past my office.

Peeling my eyes from the screen I've been staring at for the past few hours, wrapping up some much-needed work on the McDavid account, I call out, "I said I wasn't going back there."

"I need a wingman," he yells from his office.

"You said you weren't taking me back," I yell in return.

I hear a chuckle from the other side of the wall. Sure, we could use our intercom or pick up the damn phone...or walk ten feet, but what's the fun in that. "That was weeks ago. I'm sure all's forgotten. Besides, I checked the list and you're still on there."

Uh, no. I can't go to the club.

Can I?

I mean, what if Quinn is there?

Would we talk?

Would that hurt the progress we've made?

Have we made progress?

My mind goes back to Sunday and the park...and the kid. In the past, that would've been an instant turn-off. Call me a dick, but I've never been interested in women with kids. I'm not even sure I want kids. But she seems like a really good mom, and I actually like Henry. As far as kids go, he's a really cool one. And Quinn...Damn, she was even more gorgeous than the other times I've seen her. And like every time before, she left me wanting more.

"You look like you're trying to solve the national debt."

I look up to see Sebastian standing in the doorway. For someone so big, he can be stealthy.

"What's got you so puzzled?" he asks, tossing a tennis ball in the air and catching it.

"Uh, this McDavid account," I lie. Sebastian doesn't need to know I sound like a chick in my head right now. I'd never hear the end of it.

"You said you have that shit in the bag."

Rolling back from my desk, I stretch my arms over my head, needing a break. "Yeah. I mean, I do. I was just going through the last few details, making sure everything is in order."

"Yeah, okay." He watches me from the door for a few seconds, like he's going to press, but then lets it go. "So, the club. Tonight. It'll take your mind off this McDavid shit."

"I can't go." That definitely would be a bad decision. I want to see her, but the club feels all wrong. If she's there, she could be with someone else, and I might beat the shit out of the guy. If she's not there, I'll wonder if it's because of me. If she sees me and I don't see her, she might think I'm there to fuck someone else. So I definitely can't go, right?

Man up, Jude. Take your balls back and do what you fucking want.

"Is this still about her...what's her name?"

"Quinn." I love the way her name sounds and feels coming out of my mouth. I can't help but think about saying her name while pushing into her. I wonder what her face looks like when she comes. I never got to see that, only feel it and fuck if it's not the best thing I've ever felt.

"Yeah, Nurse Roland," Sebastian says, raising his eyebrows.

"Stop." I know what he's thinking about. I'm sure it's along the lines of Quinn in a skimpy nurse's uniform. I don't like him thinking about her like that. I wish he didn't even know what she looks like or what her name is. I don't like sharing her.

Fuck.

I'm so screwed.

"Okay, lover boy." Sebastian laughs with a knowing look, shaking his head.

"Get out," I yell, throwing a wadded-up piece of paper at his retreating form. Running my hands through my hair a few times and then down my face,

I groan in frustration.

What are you doing to me, Quinn Roland?

Somehow, I managed to avoid all of Sebastian's questions, inquisitions, and badgering. He wanted me to go rock climbing with him today, but I told him I had a family dinner to attend, which I do, but after the dog park. I blew him off last week using my leg as an excuse, but since it's healed up, I had to think of something new.

I look over at Fergie and shake my head at her—big ears flapping, tongue wagging. She's a happy girl. She's going to be really happy when we get to the park and she sees Henry. They've become fast friends. They have a lot in common: cuteness, energy, and fetch. I think Henry loves playing fetch as much as Fergie does.

Last week, Quinn seemed equally surprised and annoyed that I was at the park again. She doesn't know how determined and persistent I can be when I really want something. And I really want her. I want her more than I've wanted anything in my life...more than a 4.0 GPA or to win the state title in track... more than landing a job at the best advertising firm in Dallas...more than my shiny sports car. Every time she brushes me off or shuts me down, it only fuels the need for her, making me want to try harder.

This week, I brought reinforcements: donuts, chocolate milk for Henry, coffee for Quinn and me, and a new frisbee for Henry and Fergie.

When I pull into an empty parking spot close to the gate, I look around for the wild brown hair that's been starring in my dreams. I don't see it. The park is actually pretty damn empty for a Sunday. There are a couple of dogs running around, their owners lounging under shade trees or on benches, but that's about it. I decide to let Fergie out before she mauls me. After she's running free, I'll come back to the car for the donuts.

Once I'm settled on what I like to think is our regular bench now, I start to feel anxious.

Quinn and Henry still aren't here. I guess there's a good chance she could stand me up. Maybe she's not happy I keep showing up on Sundays. Maybe this is her way of telling me to fuck off. I thought we were making progress, but I've been wrong before. Lately, I've been so wrong.

Normally, I wouldn't have to work so hard for a girl's attention. Quinn makes me work double time. No, fuck that. Triple time. Just when I think she's going to soften up a little and maybe give me an inch, she throws her walls back up and shuts me out.

"Jude," a small, happy voice says from behind me, and I can't help the enormous smile that takes over my face.

"Henry," I say, turning around to find him running toward me. "Hey, dude."

"Hey, dude," he says, mimicking me and giggling.

Quinn is walking a few feet behind him, looking extra gorgeous. "You'll have to excuse him."

"You'll have to excuse him," Henry repeats.

Quinn rolls her eyes and laughs, pulling him to her. "He's got this really scary parrot disease," she says, her beautiful brown eyes growing wide. "I think I'm going to have to take him by the hospital before we go home later and let them poke him."

"No!" Henry yells, pulling away from her and running toward my girl. When Fergie sees him, she gallops over, stopping just before running into him. They have a moment on the grass, kissing and petting.

See, why can't Quinn get on board with that kind of greeting?

"The repeating is about to drive me batty this morning."

"He's been doing that all morning?" I ask, grinning over at her.

She huffs, taking a seat on the bench. "Try all week."

"Wow, that's fun," I say, trying to stifle a laugh.

"Especially when you say a bad word and forget there are little ears and your mother busts you." She presses her lips together, trying not to laugh, and rolling her eyes.

I sigh, relishing in the comfort of this absolutely normal conversation and this completely unguarded Quinn. "Oh, God. I'd get busted all the time."

"Yeah, I bet you would."

Smiling over at her, I ask incredulously, "What's that supposed to mean?"

"I've heard your filthy mouth."

She says it so casually, like she just told me the sky is blue.

I can't help the look of shock on my face. I thought that was off-limits. The night that shall not be named.

"What?" she asks, quirking an eyebrow.

I squint my eyes, trying to figure her out, but I'm afraid if I say anything, that hard stone wall she usually has up will slam into place.

"Nothing," I say, smiling. "Coffee?" I hold up the extra cup.

"Absolutely." Her expression is a mixture of surprise and...gratitude, maybe? She takes the cup and inhales deeply. "How'd you know I didn't get my second cup this morning?"

I smile and grab my own cup, taking a sip. "I was just stopping by to get some on my way here and thought I might know a beautiful brunette who would like some."

Her lips twist behind her cup. "Stop."

"What?"

"Being sweet and thoughtful."

Chuckling, I take a seat beside her, making sure to leave an appropriate amount of distance between us. "Oh, so a few minutes ago, I had a dirty mouth, and now I'm sweet and thoughtful?"

She groans. "God, that's even worse. Say something asshole-ish."

"What?" I ask, laughing.

"I need you to be a prick. Say something shitty, like you hate your mom or you ran over a bunny on the way here and laughed about it."

I can't help laughing again. She laughs too, and it's beautiful, just like everything else about her.

"I love my mom. I didn't run over a bunny. And I brought donuts." I figure now's the time for the pastry assault. My plan of attack seems to be working.

"I hate you." She grabs a donut from the open box I'm holding in front of her face and takes a bite. Not a dainty, I'm-a-girl-who-only-eats-salad kind of bite, but a let-me-cram-half-this-donut-in-my-mouth kind.

And I can't take my eyes off her mouth.

"What?" she asks, giving me a snarly look over the top of the other half of the donut she's currently inhaling. "I'm hungry." Once the donut is fully consumed, she smiles and licks her fingers to rid them of the leftover icing.

Does she know what she does to me? Is this her own personal method of torture? Does she *actually* hate me?

"I haven't eaten anything since the sandwich I had yesterday afternoon."

I frown at her admittance, not liking the idea of Quinn going without a meal or not being taken care of. And I'll put that thought away for a later date. "Why?" I ask, taking a donut and having my first bite.

"Late night at the hospital. ER was crazy," she says, leaning over me and snagging another donut.

The close contact makes my heart rate spike, and I can't stop myself from closing my eyes and inhaling deeply, taking in her hint of sweet and touch of spicy and something that is uniquely her...maybe her soap or laundry detergent. I'm not sure what it is, but I can't get enough.

"You should leave some for Henry," I tease, needing that balance of normalcy back before I do or say something to endanger this...*thing*, mood. It works, earning me a glare and a smirk.

Giving me a playful swat and making every cell in my body stand to attention, she takes a bite of her second donut. "He ate breakfast. I'm not a horrible mom."

"I can see that," I admit honestly.

She actually seems like a great mom. I like that about her.

"It's just that by the time I scrambled his eggs to perfection, he was already on my ass about coming here. To see your dog...and you," she deadpans. I can tell she's trying to be annoyed about the fact her kid likes my dog...and me, but the slight smile that sneaks up on her lips tells me she's not completely pissed about it.

"Well, I was starting to think you were going to stand me up," I say, not even thinking about the words until they're out of my mouth and I can't take them back.

Quinn stiffens a little and clears her throat, dusting her hands off. "Well, you should know that sometimes I get called in on Sundays. My schedule is very unpredictable."

I don't know if that's her way of saying "fuck off" or her way of letting me know if she's not here, it's not because she's standing me up. She's so hard for me to read, always keeping me guessing.

"Who's with Henry when you're at the hospital?" I ask, knowing I'm probably pushing my luck with this question, but it only comes from a place of genuine curiosity. But then I realize that he's probably with his dad and this was probably a bad question.

Fuck.

"My mom," Quinn says, not offering anything more than that, and I don't pry any further. But now that I've started thinking about Henry's father, I can't stop. Does she still see him? Are they a thing, or were they a thing? Why doesn't he come to the park on Sundays? Who doesn't want to spend time with a cool kid like Henry?

Quinn clears her throat again and shifts on the bench, pulling me from my inner inquisition. I'd love to ask her the questions that are on the tip of my tongue, but I'm afraid I'll scare her off. So I lounge back on the bench and stretch my legs out in front of me, trying to play it cool.

We watch Henry and Fergie play, letting a comfortable silence settle around us. Occasionally, we laugh at something they do, and Quinn comments on how good Fergie is with him. She seriously follows the kid everywhere he goes, never letting him out of her sight. I've always known she's a good dog but seeing her with Henry makes me realize how loyal and protective she is.

Later, when we're tossing the trash and I put the leash back on my girl, I try to think of something to say to Quinn. I don't want to spook her, but I want to see her again. Preferably before next Sunday.

"You should come to McNelly's tomorrow night," I tell her, swallowing the nervous lump that immediately forms in my throat once the statement is out in the open. "My friend, Sebastian, and I watch football there every Monday night. It's public. Lots of people around," I say, trying to sweeten the deal and let her know I'm not trying to get in her pants. I just want to spend time with her, get to know her better.

And of course, get in her pants again.

But I'm willing to wait for that, that's the short game.

This has now become a long game.

"I work tomorrow," she says, guiding Henry toward the parking lot.

Trying to not sound too desperate, I add, "Any Monday. I'm always there."

"Probably not a good idea." She looks down and ruffles Henry's hair.

I nod, swallowing down my disappointment. Something about today made me hope for more, but just like that, she reinforces her walls—snipping the few little threads that were becoming attached.

"Thanks for the donuts and coffee," she says, giving me a small smile.

"You're welcome."

Turning Henry toward me, she asks, "What do you say to Jude?"

"Thanks, Jude!" Henry exclaims, an adorable grin shining up at me.

"You're welcome, buddy. Maybe I'll see you next week."

She doesn't confirm nor deny that, only waves and walks Henry over to a shiny black SUV and helps him inside, buckling him in the back.

She doesn't take the beat-up Volkswagen to Sundays at the park.

Eight

ON THE DRIVE OVER TO MY MOM AND DAD'S HOUSE, I CAN'T GET
Quinn out of my mind. Part of me, the rational part, thinks I should forget
about her. It seems like all of my efforts to get her to open up are futile.
The second she lets a bit of her guard down, she puts it right back up. It
doesn't take much of anything to spook her. Just a mention of family, her job,
anything, forces her to lock up tighter than Fort Knox.

At this point, I can't imagine ever having any sort of relationship with her.

Is that what I want?

A relationship?

Yeah, I do. *I want a relationship.* With Quinn.

Even though we met under unusual circumstances, she's held my attention
since day one, or night one...fuck one. I laugh harshly to myself, shaking my
head. This whole situation is fucked up, and I should be the poster child for
why you don't go to sex clubs. The slogan could read: *Ruining cocks one phenomenal
pussy at a time...Just say no to 'no strings attached'...*The possibilities are endless.

Fun fact about me: my dad and sister are sex therapists.

I've been getting relationship and sex advice from my father since I was
eight years old and asked where babies come from. When my sister followed
in his footsteps, it really upped the uniqueness of our family. It's never a dull
moment at family dinners and they're going to have a field day with this one.

This isn't the first time I've been to a family dinner since I met Quinn,
but the last time, I had only seen her one night at the club and wasn't sure if

I'd ever see her again. So I didn't feel like bringing it up and sitting through a Keith Harris session at the dinner table. But now that I know more about her, and with each morsel of information I'm granted, I am left wanting more. I need him and his expertise. I'm hoping he'll have some light to shed...some advice, a way for me to get Quinn to trust me, anything.

I'm a desperate man.

Sighing, I wonder for the millionth time how I let myself get into this situation.

What if my dad tells me to forget her? What then? Will I? *Can* I?

Maybe he'll have some advice for that too.

Pulling into the long drive, I run a hand through my hair and down my face, rubbing my eyes roughly. The more I think about her, the more insane I start to feel...for her, about her...because of her. I try to pull myself together because I'd like to enjoy dinner before unleashing the therapist. When I see my mother peeking through the blinds, I know I can't wait any longer, so I grab the bottle of wine and bouquet of flowers I brought from the passenger seat and head inside.

"Jude," my mother sighs, pulling me into her and kissing my cheek. "Honey, you look like you've had a rough day. Did you and Sebastian work today?"

Kissing her cheek in return, I hand her the flowers and wine to take her mind off how I look.

"No, Mom. It's been a good day. I took Fergie to the park."

"Nice selection," she says, eyeing the bottle as she takes it and walks toward the kitchen.

I smile, loving her concern, but also the way she lets it drop. "Thanks, I thought it'd go well with meatloaf."

"Oh, I think it'd go well with a bologna sandwich," she says, smirking over her shoulder. My mom's not a lush, but she does love her wine. Okay, maybe she can be a lush.

After hanging my jacket by the door, I walk into the kitchen to find my parents practically making out on the island. Most people would be grossed out by that, but not me. After twenty-five years of living in the same house as Susan and Keith Harris, I'm used to it. They've always been affectionate and have never hidden it from me or my sister. I think we had our first sex talk when

I was eight. It was mostly the "women have vaginas, and men have penises" talk. When I was eleven, my dad sat me down and showed me diagrams of the female anatomy. It was scary and traumatizing, but when I was giving girls orgasms at the age of sixteen and all my friends were fumbling around with their dicks, it paid off.

To say we're all comfortable with our sexuality in this family would be an understatement.

My dad is the first to notice I'm in the room, and he stands up straight, adjusting his wire-rimmed glasses and smoothing his cardigan with a sly smile on his face. "Jude," he says nonchalantly as he walks past me.

"Good to see you too, Dad."

Going for the wineglasses, he says, "You haven't been to Sunday dinner in a couple of weeks. How's work been?"

My mom uncorks the wine and pours five glasses, draining the bottle. Lucy and Will must be joining us.

"Work's been good. Busy. We're pitching the McDavid account on Wednesday," I tell him, taking the proffered glass from my mom.

"That old man has more money than he knows what to do with. I hope they're paying you handsomely."

I shrug, taking a whiff of the wine before swirling it around in my glass. "If we get the account, it'll be my biggest one yet."

"That's my boy." My dad, looking proud, leans back in his chair as the front door opens and Lucy's chipper voice filters in from the foyer.

"Hi, baby," my mom calls out, going to her and taking the bowl she's carrying. They exchange a few words, and then I feel my sister's dainty arm wrap around my neck.

"How dare you leave us alone with these two weirdos," she whispers.

"I heard that," Dad says.

Will slaps me on the shoulder. "Hey, stranger. How's the leg?"

"All healed up," I tell him, patting my leg for proof.

Stealing a carrot from the bowl on the island, he asks, "So, are you back to incredible acts of stupidity?"

"Nah, taking it easy for another week or so, just to make sure."

"Probably a good idea," my dad says.

My mother walks back in the kitchen and pats my cheek on her way by.

"Next time, it could be your head. Or that pretty face."

"Mom." I pull back from her, rolling my eyes.

"Heaven forbid he messes up that pretty face," Will teases.

Groaning, I take a sip of my wine. "Let's stop with the pretty business and just eat. I'm starving."

We all help finish setting the table and then my dad says grace.

As we all begin to dig in, my mom pauses, sitting the salad bowl down beside my dad. Always the caretaker. "Will, did you get the final count for this weekend?"

"Looks like we're right under the two hundred mark," he says, passing the mashed potatoes.

Will and my mom have a big gig this coming weekend at the Hamilton's'. Their grandson is turning one, and Harris and Co. Celebrations is turning their backyard into a legitimate circus, like with a Ferris Wheel and ponies and clowns. The whole fucking nine yards. The money these people pay to have magazine-worthy parties for children who will never remember them is ridiculous, but it's good business for my mom and Will. They make a killing. My mom used to run the business by herself but then partnered with Will about six years ago. He had a party supply business my mom rented from, and after working together on several events, they decided to go into business together. And that's how Lucy met Will.

The rest is party-planning history.

Lucy and Will's wedding was one of the biggest in the Dallas-Fort Worth Area. People still talk about it. It was completely over the top, of course, but you know what people say: "everything's bigger in Texas", and parties thrown by the Harrises are no exception.

"So, Jude, been on any dates lately?" my sister asks, while Mom and Will are still discussing their plans for the weekend.

Lucy and my dad don't work together, but they're both very interested in my love life...too interested, if you ask me. I'm used to it, though. Between the two family love doctors and my mom and Will being nosey as fuck, there's no such thing as privacy in this house.

"Oh, yeah, son. Tell us about your latest conquest. It's been a while since you've mentioned a girl. Surely you haven't been so busy with work that it's affecting your social life," my dad goads.

See what I mean?

Usually, I don't have a problem with giving them details because I'm not a repeater when it comes to women, but now—with Quinn—I'm finding it harder to share. But who knows? Maybe they can help me think of a way to get her interested in me. They're professionals, right?

"Well, Sebastian finally got me into that sex club he's always talking about. We went a few weeks ago," I start. They already know about the club. Sebastian is a fixture around here, being my best friend since college, and he's very forthcoming about his sexual adventures, much to the enjoyment of my dad and Lucy.

"Oh, man. Really? I've always wanted to go there. Think he could get me and Lucy in?" Will asks. At first, I think he's joking, but then again, this is Will and Lucy.

When my sister squeals and throws her arms around him, I know he's totally serious. "That's how we can celebrate our anniversary," she exclaims.

Ugh, I don't even want to know about that. Adding that to my list of reasons brain bleach should be invented.

"Anyway," I continue, hoping to redirect the conversation. "After I observed a few times, I decided to get on stage and participate in an auction."

"I bet you raised the most money that night," my mom says, beaming with pride.

"With such a pretty face, how could he not?" Will jokes before I kick him under the table.

I groan, raking my fingers through my hair. *Maybe this is a bad idea.* But I'm already committed, there would be no backing out at this point, so I keep going. "I have no idea how much money was spent on me. I kind of zoned out. All I know is that I was with the most amazing woman, and I can't get her out of my head. I think I'm going crazy."

"You didn't get her phone number?" Mom asks.

"No, it's not like that. You're blindfolded while the bidding is going on, and you don't get to see who you're having sex with until you're done. It's supposed to be completely anonymous. Believe me, I tried to get her info, and she threatened to have me thrown out."

Will looks shocked and lit up with delight. "Whoa. You mean there's a woman out there that *didn't* fall for the Harris charm?"

This time, Lucy elbows her husband so I don't have to kick him again.

"Now, son, maybe you should go out with someone else. It's possible you have that night built up too much in your head, and in reality, it wasn't as great as you think. You may just need to try again with a new lady and see that it was just sex. It might be the anonymity and excitement of the bidding process that has you so...worked up."

My dad, the fucking expert. Literally.

"Keith, I can't believe you'd say that, knowing that's how we met." I swear, daggers are flying out of my mother's eyes as she glares at my dad.

I'm too pissed at what he said to even think about what my mom just announced. "It's more than that. You know I've been with my share of women—"

"And then some," Will interjects.

"Fuck off," I tell Will before continuing. "Nothing has ever compared to the time I was with Quinn. Nothing. And trust me, I've tried to get her out of my mind, but I can't."

My father smiles at my mom. "See, dear? I was just testing Jude. He seems pretty serious about her, *and* he knows her name."

Taking a deep breath, I pinch the bridge of my nose and try to relax. Just talking about her has my blood pressure rising. "Yeah, she's the one who stitched up my leg in the ER. I saw her name tag."

"So, she didn't give it to you?" I hate the way my mom's face falls when she asks, so there's no way I'm telling her about practically stalking Quinn at the hospital. It's not my finest moment and I know she wouldn't approve. Shit, in retrospect, even I don't approve. The thought of anyone, including myself, putting Quinn in an uncomfortable or threatening position makes my stomach feel sick and my hackles raise.

"Not exactly," I admit, biting back the rush of emotions about this woman I hardly know. "But it's okay now. We ran into each other at the dog park a few weeks ago and we've hung out a few times."

That puts a smile back on my mom's face. "Well, that sounds promising!"

"But," I hesitate because it's so fucking complicated. And the more I air my dirty laundry, the more I'm convinced this is a lost cause. "I'm afraid she'll turn me down if I ask her out again."

Fuck me, I sound like a whiny bitch, but this is what she does to me.

"I've never seen you this worked up over a girl before, Jude. I like it," Lucy says. "It looks like you have your work cut out for you. Just don't do anything stupid like cutting your other leg up just to see her at the hospital again." She raises her eyebrow at me, daring me to lie and say the thought hasn't entered my brain a million times by now.

Me crossing my arms over my chest and rolling my eyes at her is the only response she gets.

"It sounds like she has some walls up," my dad adds. "I'd tread carefully. But be honest with her. Show her you're a man with integrity, someone who's trustworthy and dependable." Finally, some good, applicable advice.

I'm starting to understand why Quinn is still distant at times. Henry's face comes to mind. If we start dating, it won't just be me and her. Henry is her number-one priority, and I get it. I do. I've never dated a woman with a kid before, and I won't deny being scared as shit, but I'm always up for a new adventure.

Hopefully, in this one, we'll all have fun and no one will get hurt.

"Thanks. I really appreciate your input, but I need to backtrack for a minute." I turn and look at my mother. "Mom, I thought Uncle Mark introduced you to Dad?"

"Oh, well, he did...in a manner of speaking." She fidgets with her fingers, and I can't remember the last time I've seen my mother nervous. She and my dad have always been honest—sometimes too honest—with us about their relationship. "We met at a Greek function at our university that was being sponsored by your father and uncle's fraternity. Mark did introduce us...right before your father went on stage for a bachelor auction." She blushes before she continues. "I won him."

"Why would you keep that part of the story a secret?" Lucy asks.

Mom blushes a little and I'm completely taken aback. She stares at her wineglass and then at my father. "I don't know. I guess I thought it would be too shocking for you."

"You took me to a sex shop where there were dildos the size of my forearm for my eighteenth birthday, yet you didn't think I could handle learning you bid on Dad for your first date?" Leave it to Lucy to pull out the big guns.

The entire table is howling with laughter at this point.

"All right, fine! It was a stupid secret to keep," my mother admits, wiping the corners of her eyes. "But it was the best two hundred dollars I ever spent."

"I bet the frat could've raised even more money if sex had been part of the deal, huh, Jude?" My dad winks at me, and I'm actually thankful to have such understanding parents. It'll make this thing with Quinn go a lot more smoothly, *if* I can ever get her to agree to a date and my parents don't scare her off.

My mom smiles, swatting at my dad. "What are you complaining about, Keith? You had plenty of sex that night, and you've been getting it ever since. I got a bargain, I tell ya!"

Due to growing up with these two as parents, I never really understood the big deal about sex. It's always been discussed as freely as the weather in our house. It wasn't until I was a teenager and my friends started talking about it that I realized my parents were a different breed.

"No complaints from me," my dad retorts with a wink. "I'll show you just how non-complaining I am as soon as we kick our children out."

Keith and Susan Harris, ladies and gentlemen.

Nine

"WHAT'S GOT YOU ALL RILED UP?" SEBASTIAN ASKS AS I CHUG MY second beer.

It's not even two minutes into the first quarter of the Colts and Panthers game, and I honestly couldn't give two shits about who wins. Normally, I pace myself and drink a beer a quarter, unless the Cowboys are playing. Then it's a totally different ballgame. Sebastian and I usually have to take Tuesdays off when the Cowboys play on Monday nights, especially if they lose.

I set my empty mug on the bar in front of me and glance back at the door. "I might've mentioned to Quinn that we come here every Monday night," I say, trying to sound nonchalant about it.

"Did you invite her?" he asks, giving me a half-smile before taking a sip of his beer.

I don't want to commit to the fact I invited her because then I'm going to look like the pathetic loser I am when she doesn't show. "Maybe," I finally say.

"You either did or you didn't."

Glancing over at the door for the millionth time, I admit, "I told her she should come."

"And what did she say?"

"She blew me off, like she does every time I try to ask her out or try to get to know her better."

My frustration with this is growing exponentially by the second. Something has to give. Or I need a fucking lobotomy.

"This woman knows how to play hard to get. I'll give her that."

"I don't think it's just that," I tell him, letting out a deep sigh. "I think there's something else there. Her guard is always up."

"You said she has a kid," Sebastian says, leaning on the bar. "Maybe she's just being protective?"

"Yeah, maybe." The walls she has up could be because of Henry, but I still feel like there's more to the story. In fact, I know there is. Like, where's Henry's dad? *Who* is Henry's dad? Does she still see him? Have feelings for him? And there's also that nagging thought that's recently joined the cacophony in my brain: *what if she's married?*

There's so much I don't know about Quinn Roland.

Sebastian turns his attention away from the large screen in front of us and levels me with his stare. "Are you more nervous she's going to show up or that she's going to blow you off?"

"Don't mention blowing and Quinn in the same sentence," I say with a laugh, trying to diffuse some of the tension in my body. "My blue balls can't take it."

"You're avoiding the question."

I divert my gaze back to the game and start picking at a plate of cheese fries sitting between us. "I don't know, dude. Both, I guess."

I want her to show up, but if she does, then what?

"Man, she's got you so twisted." Sebastian snickers, shaking his head.

We sit and drink a couple more beers while watching the Panthers get the shit beat out of them. I continuously check the door, much to Sebastian's amusement.

After our halftime dart game, we settle back in at our spot at the bar. I glance at my watch and see that it's after nine and wonder what Quinn's doing, if she's working or at home. For the millionth time over the past month, I wish I had her number.

A catcall coming from the back of the bar makes me turn around to see a gorgeous brunette walk through the front door.

My gorgeous brunette.

Quinn flips the guy the bird. I smirk, watching her walk past the table and then scan the room. The fact she's here makes my heart beat double-time. When her eyes meet mine, I swear a hint of a smile forms on her lips. She raises an eyebrow as if to say "I'm here", like she's not sure what she's doing or if she should be here...but she's here.

What now?

I slide off the barstool and meet her halfway.

"Hey," I say, walking up to her and slipping my hands in my pockets to keep myself from reaching out and pulling her to me.

"Hey," she says, looking around the bar. There's something different about her. Her hair is in the messy bun I've seen her wear at the hospital, and she's dressed in jeans and a sweater. Nothing out of the ordinary. I look down to see the combat boots firmly in place, like her armor, laced halfway up with the remainder of the laces wrapped around her ankles. When I make my way back up to her face, that's when I see it—the slight hint of nervousness. She bites the corner of her mouth and her eyes continue to dance around the room. I can see the internal battle of her wondering if she's making a mistake.

"Wanna drink?" I ask, hoping to ease her nerves.

"Yeah," she says with a hard laugh. "I could really use one."

I guide her to the bar, walking behind her and turning my head toward the guys she flipped off when she came in. My death glare lets them know in no uncertain terms to back the fuck off.

As far as they're concerned, or anyone else in this bar, she's mine.

"What can I get ya, honey?" Jimmy asks.

"A shot of 1800," Quinn says, sliding onto the barstool I'd been occupying.

I lean against the bar beside her and watch as Sebastian's smile grows wider. He's eating this shit up with a spoon. The look he gives me over the top of her head is one of shock and amusement.

"Quinn, this is Sebastian." I nod to the other side of her, gesturing to the beast.

Sebastian turns in his seat and offers her his hand.

"Sebastian, Quinn."

Quinn's shoulders relax a little. "Ah, yes. I remember you from the ER. One of the nurses had to give you something for your nausea. Wasn't it bad sushi or something like that?" she asks.

He clears his throat and winces.

"Bad sushi?" I ask, not sure what she's talking about. We haven't had sushi for a couple of months. The place we usually go to closed down.

"Yeah," Sebastian says nervously, and I can see the lie all over his face.

I laugh and shake my head. "Fucking pussy," I mutter under my breath.

"What?" Quinn asks, looking back and forth at the two of us.

"He gets sick at the sight of blood," I tell her.

Quinn laughs and turns her attention back to Sebastian. "So that whole bad fish thing was a big ol' fat lie, huh?"

Sebastian's cheeks pink up a little. "Yes, okay?" He stares at me. "Happy now?"

"Extremely." I love to see him squirm.

When Jimmy returns with Quinn's shot, she slams it back and slides the glass back to him. "I'll have one more. Then a Coke, straight," she instructs.

"Bad night in the ER?" I ask, watching her.

"Yeah." She lets out a deep breath and rubs her eyes, and I start to ask more but refrain. She's here, and that's enough for now. I don't want to scare her off.

When Jimmy sets her second shot down in front of her with a grin, she looks over at Sebastian. "Lots and lots of blood," she says teasingly, tossing the tequila back.

Sebastian shakes his head and laughs, taking a drink of his beer.

We watch the rest of the game. Quinn and Sebastian exchange jabs, and I sit back and enjoy the free entertainment. When the game is over, Sebastian asks for his tab, and I slap some money down on the bar to cover mine and Quinn's. She gives me a glare but doesn't argue. Maybe I should've let her pay so she'd want to come back and hang out again, but I couldn't. I have all sorts of weird feelings when it comes to Quinn, and one is the need to take care of her. I've never felt that way about anyone, but it hits me so strongly sometimes.

"I'm gonna head out," Sebastian says, slapping me on the back. "Quinn, it was a pleasure to see you again. See you tomorrow, Jude." He waves as he walks out of the bar.

Leaning down until my lips are close to her ear—because I just fucking need it, I need to be close to her...have a little something to take with me until I can see her again—I ask, "Can I walk you to your car?"

Standing up, she starts to walk toward the door, and I think she's going to leave me standing there like a fool, but she stops to toss a look over her shoulder. "You coming?"

It takes me a minute to get myself together. She's looking at me with a spark in her eyes, and the confidence she usually wears like a cloak is back in full force. When I finally get my feet to work, I have to jog to catch up to her.

"Thanks for coming tonight," I tell her as we start to cross the street. I look around for the black SUV she was driving on Sunday, but it's not there. Instead, it's the beat-up red Volkswagen parked a few feet away

"Yeah, uh, thanks for inviting me," she says, but it sounds more like a question than a statement. She digs in her bag and pulls out keys. "It was a really bad day in the ER, and I needed...something."

I start to wonder if I hadn't invited her here, would she have gone to the club instead? Maybe that's what she usually does to blow off some steam.

"Do you want to come to my apartment?" I ask before I have a chance to stop myself.

Her head snaps around, and she gives me a pointed look, similar to the one she's given me at the club. Almost a *fuck off* or *in your fucking dreams*. She walks closer to her car and unlocks the door. After she tosses her purse inside, she turns and leans back against the car. "I don't do relationships."

The definitiveness in her voice lets me know she's not playing. It's not an excuse or an out. It's a fact.

I nod and shove my hands into my front pockets, rocking back on my heels. "Okay," I tell her, waiting for whatever she's going to say next. I'll take whatever she'll give me. We don't have to do a relationship. As long as she doesn't tell me to go fuck myself, we're good.

"Not at your apartment," she finally says.

My mind races. *Is she saying yes? To sex? With me?* I look around and try to think fast.

"And not here," she laughs, shaking her head.

"Right. Of course not." I clear my throat and say the first thing that comes to mind. "What about the hotel down the street?"

"That works. I need to do something first, but I can meet you there in half an hour."

With my heart beating wildly in my chest, I act on impulse. "I'll text you the room number."

She holds out her hand, and at first, I'm not sure what she wants. "Phone," she demands.

"Oh, right," I say, pulling it out of my pocket and handing it to her.

And that, my friends, is how you get Quinn Roland's phone number.

Taking the phone back from her, I look at her info on the screen and inwardly fist-pump myself. Outwardly, I play it cool and slip my phone back into my pocket, nodding my head.

She doesn't say anything else, just nods her head back at me and climbs in the driver's seat. Next thing I know, she's pulling away, and I'm left standing there...dumbfounded.

Did that just happen?

Are we really doing this?

Half an hour later, I'm nervously bouncing my leg as I sit on the edge of the bed at the Omni Hotel and watch my phone like a pot of water I'm waiting to boil. I texted her the room number, but she hasn't replied. It's only been a few minutes, but the thought that she could stand me up is consuming me.

Not being able to wait any longer, I stand up and head for the door. My nerves are shot, and I feel like a lion trapped in a cage. I need space. I need to step out of this room before I drive myself crazy.

Hopefully, I'll catch Quinn as she walks into the lobby.

I pull the door open and stop short. A very quiet, very unsure Quinn is standing on the other side of the hallway. Her eyes are wide and nervous, and she's toying with the hem of her sweater. With her presence, my body finally relaxes. I don't like seeing her so apprehensive, but at least she's here. I slowly reach for her hand and guide her into the room.

Once we're inside and the door is closed, Quinn lets out a deep breath. She seems more comfortable now, like walking into this room was the hardest part. I'm not sure what to think about that. I'm just relieved she's here.

"Can I get you anything to drink?" I ask, walking over to the mini bar to occupy myself.

"No, thanks. I'm fine. Sorry it took me so long. I went home to say goodnight to Henry, and then when I got here, I had to stop myself from running away."

Ouch.

"This is why I like going to the club. There are no expectations and I don't have to talk if I don't want to. I get in, get what I want, and get out. This—"

She moves her hand back and forth between us. "This is new to me."

The fact we're talking—*she's* talking—is enough to set me at ease a little. If she's talking, it means she's not running.

"You said you don't do relationships, so...what do you want, Quinn?"

I'm willing to give her just about anything she wants at this point. "You want to release some tension? Let me make you feel good. If you don't do relationships, we'll keep it simple, just like at the club. Just sex."

She chews on her bottom lip while she thinks. Finally, she looks up at me with a small smile on her face. "Yeah, that'd be great, actually. But only if you're okay with it. I know we don't know each other very well, but in case you haven't noticed, I have a hard time letting people into my life."

I can't stop the laughter that shoots out of my mouth. I worry about pissing her off, but when I see her roll her eyes at me before giggling, I know she's fine.

"That's a fucking understatement, Quinn, but it's cool. I get that you want to protect yourself, as well as your son."

She gives me a soft smile for a split second, softer than I've seen from her and it makes my heart flip in my chest. "Thanks," she says, taking a step closer to me. The energy in the room starts to spark. "I don't want you to get your hopes up that this will evolve into something more, Jude. This does not mean we're dating. You can't show up at my work. Don't send me flowers. No phone calls. Just sex."

I step closer until we're face to face with nothing between us. "Got it." I lower my mouth to hers, preparing to seal the deal with a kiss when she puts her hand between us as a barrier.

"No kissing. It's too personal."

What is this, *Pretty Woman*? Fuck that.

Reaching out to tuck a few wayward strands of hair behind her ear, looking for any excuse to touch her, I offer a rebuttal. "If you remember, we've already kissed. And it was fantastic, best fucking kiss of my life. I've been dying to kiss you again for weeks. Seeing you at the park and not being able to touch you... taste you." I pause, leaning down I place a soft kiss on her neck and then swipe my tongue out. "It's been pure torture. Don't tell me you haven't thought about it...wanted to do it again. Are you really going to deny—"

Before I can finish, she attacks me.

Her mouth and tongue claiming me while her nails leave trails of the most beautiful kind of destruction on my skin. She's ravenous and wild, and I fucking love she wants me as much as I want her.

I must have blacked out at some point because I have no recollection of my shirt being taken off. Maybe I was just mesmerized by the feel of Quinn in my arms again. When her hands grab for my belt buckle, I stop her.

"Slow down. I want to undress you," I tell her. My voice is deep, raspy even, but she complies with my request. Since I was blindfolded the last time we were together, I've only had my imagination to fill in this part.

Carefully, I remove her sweater and toss it on the nearby chair. Her breasts are practically spilling out of her bra, especially since she's breathing so heavily, but I force my attention to her jeans, undoing the fly and pulling them down her legs. Squatting down, I finish removing the denim from her body and place soft kisses on her thighs and stomach before standing back up.

Quinn watches every step, and the lust darkening her eyes is impossible to miss. I lean down and kiss her again. This kiss has more control but just as much intensity as the one before, and I swear I could kiss this woman forever.

My hands travel to her back and I swiftly unhook her bra. Quinn wastes no time pulling the straps off and letting the material fall to the floor.

In all my life, I've never seen a pair of tits more perfect than these. I've daydreamed about Quinn's breasts so much over the last few weeks, I almost want to pinch myself to make sure this moment is really happening. Instead, I pinch *her*. Rolling her nipples firmly with my fingers, I tug them a bit before I let my mouth envelop her puckered flesh, remembering how delicious she tastes.

Quinn's nails scratch at my scalp while holding my head in place. "Jude," she moans. "Fuck me. Now. Please."

I want to so bad. I've had tunnel vision since that night at the club, only focusing on how to get Quinn back into my bed...any bed. Now that it's finally happening, I want to savor every minute.

"Not yet," I tell her, meeting her eyes and the opposition that is strong in them.

Before she can argue, I explain. "I didn't get to *see* you the night we met. Granted, being blindfolded made the sex very intense, but I wish I could've seen you...your body move against mine...your face as you came. I want that now."

"But you can see me. I don't understand what more you want," she argues.

"Yes, I can see you, and you're the sexiest woman I've ever laid eyes on. But I also want to watch you."

She quirks an eyebrow. "Watch me?"

"Yeah, I want to watch you touch yourself. I want to watch you make yourself come, and then *I'm* going to make you come."

Her breathing starts to pick up, and she bites her bottom lip before sliding her lace panties to the floor. "Okay."

Holy shit.

I didn't know if she'd agree or not, and I really don't know how I'm going to manage watching her and not touching her, but I'll do my damnedest to keep my hands to myself. Because I really fucking want this.

I want everything with this woman.

Quinn crawls onto the bed and immediately starts caressing her tits. She licks her fingertips before pulling and twisting her nipples just like I was doing earlier.

I knew she liked that.

As I sit at the end of the bed, my dick is hard as a rock pressed against the zipper of my jeans, begging for release. But not yet. The last thing I want is to blow my load before getting inside Quinn.

Her eyes never leave mine as she lies back, propping herself up on a stack of pillows.

"You're so fucking beautiful," I murmur, running my hands up my thighs to keep from reaching out and touching her. Her eyes flutter closed as she slips one hand down her body and then presses her middle finger between her folds.

Swallowing hard, I adjust my dick and lick my lips as she spreads her legs wider.

I'm pretty sure I've died and gone to heaven.

"Fuck." *Fuck this.* I can't take it any longer. I need to be inside her. Now. Jumping off the bed, I quickly discard my jeans. There's a good chance I will die in this hotel room if I ignore my cock any longer.

Quinn giggles at my hasty action, then she presses two fingers inside her pussy and lets out the most erotic sigh I've ever heard. When she pulls out, I can see her glistening fingers and my balls start to tighten.

"You're so wet, Quinn. Fuck, you're driving me crazy."

I'm mesmerized by the sight of Quinn giving herself pleasure. She's not shy, and she knows exactly how and where to touch to make herself feel good. I want to know her body that well and maybe, just maybe, teach her a few new tricks.

When she pushes her fingers back inside, my hand automatically goes to my cock and squeezes. With her back arching, her moans grow louder and louder as she continues to pleasure herself.

"That's it, Quinn. Make yourself come."

Her eyes snap open at my demand and she licks her lips. "You too," she gasps. "Come on my tits. Hurry."

No way am I turning down that request.

Within seconds, I'm on my knees next to her, dick in hand, pumping it with quick strokes.

Even after everything I've experienced sexually, *this* is the most erotic thing I've ever done. It's raw yet intimate, and I feel like we're becoming bonded beyond our bodies right now.

"I'm coming, Jude. Oh, god!"

Watching her body tense and pulse and spasm as she groans so loud I'm sure everyone on this floor can hear her, causes my orgasm to rip through me, painting white ribbons over her chest and stomach.

She lies there, satiated for a moment, sighing as the last of her orgasm fades. I fall onto the bed next to her and let the blood flow back to other parts of my body, wondering what the fuck just happened.

Damn, that was fast.

When I glance over and see Quinn rubbing my cum into her skin, I feel my dick twitch. He knows that's fucking hot. Seeing myself on her and her liking it is just the catalyst I need to be ready for more.

"That was..." Quinn drifts off and rolls onto her side, her soft bare leg tangling with mine.

"Yeah," I agree, pulling her closer.

Last time, she bolted. But not this time. This time, I'm gonna get my round two.

Ten

As I push into her, staring down at her gorgeous face, I'm having trouble believing this is real life.

Still.

Even after watching her pleasure herself and coming all over her, I still find myself needing reassurance this isn't some vivid dream. But this is more than a production or a performance; it's more than her buying me off an auction block.

Somewhere between her walking through the hotel door and being under me, things changed. She might not want to admit it, but I feel it. I feel it in the way her hands are grasping and clinging to my back. I feel it in the way her thighs are squeezing my torso, begging for more. I feel it in the way she's looking at me right this moment, biting her lip to keep from crying out. But it doesn't work.

It's loud.

It's mutual.

It's fucking phenomenal.

If I thought our first sexual encounter changed my life, this one is rearranging my future. There's no way I'm going to be able to be just a fuck buddy.

No way.

"Oh, God," she says on a moan, close to crying. "Fuck."

"Yeah, baby. That's what we're doing," I tell her, leaning down toward her ear and biting gently on her lobe.

Her nails scratch my back as she digs in deeper. "Harder," she pleads, but she doesn't have to. I'll give her anything she wants. Any fucking thing.

As sweat beads up on my forehead, I thrust harder, giving her the friction she desires. Looking down, I'm glad we kept the lights on. I missed out on so much the first time. I love seeing the desperation in her eyes, knowing she's as into this as I am. The blindfold was great, but this is better.

"You're so beautiful," I tell her, chasing my breath.

Her mouth falls open, like she's going to say something, but all that comes out is a satisfied moan before her eyes fall shut and she pushes her head farther into the pillow.

I take the opportunity to feast on her neck, tasting and nipping, letting my lips hover around the base near her shoulder.

She moves her hands from my back to my hair and pulls tight, crying out as I rock harder against her.

There's no barrier except for the condom on my dick. Nothing between us but the sweat dripping from our bodies. I don't want to come yet. I want this to last, so I switch positions, rolling onto my back and taking her with me. Her hands press into my chest as she creates her own rhythm—riding me, owning me.

"Do whatever feels good, Quinn. I want to see you come. I want to see that beautiful face when you fall apart on top of me."

Taking my words as her cue, she does just that. She uses me for her pleasure. I grip her hips, my fingertips digging into her soft skin, encouraging her to be as fast and hard as she needs to get off. Before long, she tightens around me as her entire body trembles and she completely comes undone. I lean up, holding her to me, allowing her to ride out her orgasm. It takes a few minutes, but she slowly comes back to me.

I push the damp hair from her face and look into her eyes. Something about this—the position, the closeness—feels too right, too vulnerable. With a hooded gaze, she watches me. I think about pulling out and finishing myself off in the bathroom because I'm not sure if she wants to continue. She looks spent, and I don't want to take any more than she wants to give. But before I can move her off me, she pushes up and sits back on her heels, giving me the most glorious view of her hot, slick center and her flushed tits. She looks wild, feral, and freshly fucked. It's her best look yet. She's always beautiful, but I'd like to keep her this way 24/7.

Me.

Her.

No one else.

Just us.

Waiting for her cue, I sit there, my dick at full attention. Her eyes travel down my body, and she smirks at my cock before looking me in the eye. "How do you want me?" she asks boldly.

Holy fuck.

I swallow hard. "On your hands and knees," I tell her without thinking.

Giving me a wicked smile, she climbs to the center of the bed with her ass in the air.

I take a moment to say a prayer of gratitude and then take a deep breath to keep from blowing my load before I get back inside her.

Dead puppies.

Saggy grandma titties.

I line up to her entrance and slide in. It's hot and wet and fucking heaven. For a second, I just bask in the goodness of Quinn's pussy until I have to move. With my hands gripping her round ass tightly, I pull back and then slam back in, watching myself enter her over and over.

Her choppy breaths and screams of pleasure spur me on. When she turns her head around to watch, I lose it. With short quick thrusts, I come so hard and long, my vision blurs.

Quinn falls onto her elbows, and it takes all my strength to hold myself off her. Leaning back on my heels, I pull out and carefully roll the condom off. Barely making it off the bed without face-planting, I toss the condom in the trash and then fall back down on the bed beside Quinn.

We lie there, breathing, letting our heads come back from wherever they've been.

After a few minutes, she slowly rolls toward me, and I feel her eyes on me.

I guess we should talk.

"So, how do we do this?" I ask, running my hand through my hair. I don't want to come off too needy, so I try to play her game. Keep things casual.

"I have your number," she says, rolling onto her back and staring at the ceiling. "I'll text you."

Needing to see her face, I turn on my side. "And what if I can't make it?"

She shrugs before answering. "That's fine."

"What if I want to see you?" I ask.

"Then you can text me."

The fact she's giving me permission to text her—albeit for sex—is a huge step in the right direction. Contact with her, in any shape or form, is what I want.

"What should I say?" I ask, not wanting to mess this up before we even get started.

"Emergency."

I laugh, trying to make light of this arrangement we're making, but thinking of this in a casual manner doesn't sit well with me. "Okay."

"And if I can't make it," she adds, giving me a sly smile. "I'll text back, 'call 911'."

This time, my laugh is real.

She looks at me and her eyes are light and carefree. "And we meet here," she says. "If I text you, I'll pay for the room. If you text me, you pay for the room."

"What about Sundays?" I ask, feeling a rock thud as it drops into the pit of my stomach when she turns her head towards me. The sparkle in her eyes fades and the seriousness returns.

She looks at me hard as her teeth come down on her bottom lip. "I guess we can still do Sundays at the park," she says tentatively. "On one condition."

"Whatever you want," I tell her, because not seeing Henry would really suck. I'm trying to keep the desperation out of my voice, but I think I'm failing.

Her features soften for a moment, but then her eyebrows squeeze together, like she's thinking really hard. "Don't get attached, okay?"

It's a gut punch for sure, but I pretend like it's not. "No," I shake my head, more for myself than her. "I'm not. I just...well, Fergie really loves playing with Henry. She doesn't get much outside time because I'm always working and sh—"

"It's fine, Jude," she says, cutting off my embarrassing ramble. "Henry really loves it too. I just don't want to muddy the waters."

"No mud. I promise."

"Where do you work?" she asks, like it just dawned on her she doesn't know. "You know where I work, so I think it's only fair that I know where you work."

Tit for tat. Is that how it is? I smile, kind of loving I have something over on her, but it fades quickly because unlike her, I want her to know everything about me...my job, my family, where I see myself in five years. But I start with my job. "I work for Wallace Advertising."

She nods her head. "Advertising," she says, mulling it over. "So, what exactly do you do?"

"Right now, we're getting ready to pitch our sales campaign idea to McDavid."

"The big car dealership?" she asks, sliding off the bed and gathering her clothes.

"Yep. Our meeting is this Wednesday," I tell her, looking at the time and knowing I need to get home. Speaking of McDavid reminds me that Sebastian and I still have a lot of work ahead of us tomorrow to prepare for the meeting.

"Is that a pretty big account?" She walks into the bathroom, and I can't help but watch her as she goes—her ass bouncing perfectly and her dark hair swaying loosely down her back.

I clear my throat and my thoughts, forcing myself back into the conversation. "One of the biggest I've worked on so far."

"That's good. Do you like it?" she asks loudly, splashing water on her face and then drying it with a towel. When she walks back out, her hair is once again twisted up in a bun.

"I do. It's competitive, and the environment is always changing. I love a challenge, and advertising offers plenty of those. We have season tickets for the Oilers on the line with this one." I pull my jeans on, stuffing my still semi-erect cock into the confines. I think as long as I'm in the vicinity of Quinn, I'll always be somewhat hard. It's like a law of physics or some shit.

"Oh, I see. A little side bet to sweeten the deal." She smiles as she slips her own jeans on.

Grabbing my shirt from beside the bed, I yank it over my head. "Yeah, our boss knows how to dangle the carrot in front of us."

"You keep saying we and us. Do you have a partner?"

"Yeah, I've been working with Sebastian on this campaign."

Fastening her bra and hiding her fabulous tits, she asks, "Really? That big guy is in advertising?"

As each piece of her body gets covered, I miss it.

"Sebastian is fierce. I know he comes off like a big kid, but he's really good at his job."

Grabbing my shoes, I realize how domestic this all feels, dressing together and having a normal conversation. *Don't get attached.* Right.

"You two are tight," she says from behind her shirt before she slips it over her head.

I smile at the way her hair gets a little messed up, loving the look on her. She's perfectly imperfect and I find my heart squeezing when our eyes meet. Clearing my throat, I reply, "Yeah, we've been friends forever. Long before Wallace."

"That's nice." She smiles softly and slips her feet into the combat boots.

"Yeah." I stand there, fully dressed, wishing like hell we could rewind and go back to me opening the door and her standing there. I want to do it all over again...and again...and again.

"Well," she says, putting her bag on her shoulder and slipping her phone into her pocket. "I guess I should go."

"Yeah," is all I can say. I want to say so much more, but I don't. More would scare her off. More would close the tiny bit of space she's allowed me in. More would send us back to being mere acquaintances. So I'll bide my time, and I'll take what she can give me. For now. "I'll walk you to your car."

As we walk out the door and into the hall, I put my hand on the small of her back, and she tenses slightly. It's small, but I feel it, so I drop my hand and settle for walking close to her.

"So, how'd you get into nursing?" I ask, trying to make small talk and hold on to her presence just a little while longer.

"Uh, my dad," she replies, but I feel the weight in her words, and something tells me there's more there. "And I'm not a nurse. I'm a physician's assistant."

"Oh, I just saw your name badge that night I was in the ER and assumed..." I say, walking onto the elevator behind her.

"Yeah, I was going for my MD, but stuff happened...life," she says, trailing off, not saying too much. Her head dips forward, and I watch her as she watches her feet. When the elevator stops on the ground floor, we step out into the quiet, empty lobby. At this time of night, not many people are checking in or out of the Omni. "Anyway, I changed courses and became a PA. It's good. It allows me to work in the ER, which is something I've always wanted. It's fast-paced and challenging."

"Kinda like advertising," I say, smiling.

She offers me a small smile in return and nods. "Yeah, I guess so."

"Well, this is me," she says, pointing to the beat-up Volkswagen.

"I had fun tonight," I tell her, feeling my cheeks heat up with the admission.

Unlocking the car, she tosses her bag into the passenger seat. "Me too...I'll see you later."

"Sunday, if not before," I add, not ready to let her go.

She nods and gets in the car. "Hope you have a good meeting on Wednesday."

"Thanks." I smile and watch as she closes the door, only to roll down the window. "What constitutes an emergency?" I ask, bracing my hands against the car door.

She twists her lips to keep from smiling. "I'll let you be the judge of that."

"Keep your phone handy," I say with a wink.

She rolls her eyes and laughs. Without another word, she drives away, once again leaving me watching her tail lights and wishing she was still here...always leaving me wanting more.

Eleven

WEDNESDAY MORNING, SEBASTIAN STRIDES INTO MY OFFICE WEARING his power suit, complete with a silk tie and cufflinks. I can see in his eyes he's ready to win this account, and I'm confident he can see the same in mine. "How long have you been here?"

"Since six. I was so hyped up I couldn't sleep any longer." I lean over the pool table and knock the eight ball into the corner pocket before immediately setting up for another game.

To be honest, today's pitch for the McDavid account wasn't the only thing keeping me up. I haven't seen nor heard from Quinn since our night at the hotel, and I feel like I'm losing my mind. It's only been a couple of days, but now that I've had her—*really* had her—I need more. *Now.* However, my stubborn side isn't letting me give in too soon.

Sebastian grabs his pool stick and breaks the balls, landing a striped ball in a pocket. "We *so* got this, Jude. I even bought myself a personalized Oilers jersey last night as an early congratulations present."

I'm not normally a superstitious guy, but my stomach flips, a bit worried we might be too cocky.

But when I think about all of the hard work Sebastian and I have done on this pitch, I relax again. It seemed daunting at first, coming up with a new ad campaign for one of the biggest car dealerships in the country, but once we started working on it, the great ideas started flowing. Mr. McDavid would be an idiot to not choose us.

There's a knock on my office door before Sheila, our office assistant, enters.

"Good morning. I just wanted to let you know that the conference room is set up with everything you need for the presentation and Mr. McDavid's secretary called to say he's on his way. He should be here in about twenty minutes."

"Thanks, Sheila. We'll be ready," I assure her. She nods her head and leaves while I sink a solid ball in a side pocket.

After our game, I put on my suit jacket and run my fingers through my hair, hoping to tame it some. Professional appearances are important in this business, and I don't want Mr. McDavid to think we're too young or inexperienced to handle his account.

We're in the conference room ready to start when McDavid arrives. He shakes our hands and sits at the head of the table before telling us his vice president of sales is running a bit late but will be here soon.

"Not a problem, Mr. McDavid," Sebastian tells him. "Would you care to look over our portfolio while we wait?"

"That's quite all right, son. I've done my homework on you two, and I'm very interested in what your ideas are for my company."

"Excellent." Sebastian beams as he rubs his large hands together. "Jude and I are confident you'll be pleased with what we have in store for you and the future of David McDavid Automotive."

While Sebastian and Mr. McDavid engage in a conversation that covers trucks, football, and where to get the best steak, I zone out and think about Quinn again.

I can't figure her out, and it drives me crazy. I know we're supposed to be casual—fuck buddies or whatever—but the more I'm with her, the more I want. Not just her body, either. I want everything, to know everything.

The clues she gives me—the things she says and does—they make no sense.

Her job, her son, the club, two very different vehicles, and those fucking combat boots.

The way she bites her lip to hide her smile from me, her smoldering eyes, her laugh, and the way she moans my name when I'm inside her.

What does it all mean?

Fuck. Now is not the time to let myself get distracted.

I walk to the corner of the room and pour myself a glass of water. Sebastian and Mr. McDavid are still going on about whether Ronny Torro will survive the next football season when the door opens, allowing a very tall, very blonde woman to walk in.

"Sorry I'm late, Mr. McDavid, gentlemen," she says, addressing the room with confidence. She gives me a polite smile and a nod of her head before turning to do the same to Sebastian.

When her eyes reach him, though, her face hardens briefly before a fake grin appears.

What the hell?

Looking at Sebastian, I notice he's gone deathly pale. I don't even think the guy's blinking. As much as I can't wait to find out what the fuck is going on, we have an account to win.

"Boys, this is my shining star, Lexie Jameson. If I hire you, the three of you will be working very closely during this campaign, so I thought she should sit in on your presentation."

"That's a great idea," I say, glancing over at Sebastian and silently telling him to get his shit together. "It's nice to meet you, Mrs. Jameson. I'm Jude Harris." I offer my hand, and she takes it in her firm grasp, shaking it, showing she means business.

"Thank you, Mr. Harris. It's *Ms.* Jameson, actually." She turns a hard glare to Sebastian and asks, "And you are?"

Watching my best friend stammer and sweat in front of a woman is quite entertaining, and it doesn't happen nearly as often as it should. He finally pushes away from the table and stands, indiscreetly wiping his hand on the leg of his slacks before offering it to Ms. Jameson.

"I'm Sebastian, ma'am. Sebastian Jones. It's a pleasure to be in your presence, ma'am. I mean, Miss...uh, Lexie...Jameson. Yeah, Lexie, that's you. Lexie Jamison, mmhmm."

Fuck.

The words rush from his mouth, and I want to crawl under the table and die from secondhand embarrassment. If he fucks this up, I'll kill him.

Thankfully, Mr. McDavid finds the whole encounter thoroughly entertaining and begins howling with laughter. So much so, he's soon pulling a handkerchief out of his breast pocket to dab at his eyes.

"Simmer down, Mr. Jones. You're not the first person my Lexie has had this effect on, and I dare say, you won't be the last. It's one of the many reasons I hired her. Her beauty and brains make for a killer combination, wouldn't you agree?"

Sebastian simply nods his head, still staring at Lexie. When he finally tries to speak, I notice the way his mouth gapes, but nothing comes out. I can't take it anymore. There's no way in hell I'm going to let him ruin this for us, so I stand and grip his shoulder firmly as I make my way to the head of the table. "Thank you for the opportunity to pitch our campaign ideas to you this morning, Mr. McDavid. And Ms. Jameson, I'm so glad you could join us. I hope this is the beginning of a wonderful working relationship."

I smooth the front of my suit, making sure my tie is tucked neatly inside my jacket. As Sebastian clears his throat, I cut my eyes at him, silently telling him to sit there and let me handle it, but his eyes are trained across the table to the leggy blonde. She's also not hearing a word I'm saying, her icy blue glare shooting over at Sebastian.

As the two of them battle it out in a stare-down of epic proportions, I continue the pitch Sebastian and I have been working on for the past few months, hoping I can impress Mr. McDavid enough to give us the account.

Smiling, I pick up the remote control. "Let's get started, shall we?" I ask as I flip to the first visual aide.

Sebastian is so paying for this little stunt. He knows the rules: you never fuck the competition, you never fuck the clients, and if for some reason you break rules one and two, you never bring that shit into the boardroom.

He's obviously broken two of those rules.

"Jude, my boy," Mr. McDavid says, shaking my hand and clapping my shoulder all at the same time. "That was one of the best spiels I've ever heard. Shit, I'd buy a fleet of cars after hearing your campaign."

"Well, thank you, Mr. McDavid," I tell him, smiling as I return his firm handshake. "We look forward to working with you and for you, sir."

"I wasn't sure the two of you could handle this. I have to admit I was a little hesitant when I heard Frank and Joe had handed this off, but I see why they put so much confidence in you." His distinguished gray mustache twitches as he smiles. "I heard about the little side wager you two had going. How about I sweeten the deal with a box suite?"

My smile grows, and I glance over to Sebastian, who seems to be back in control of his faculties. His eyes widen, and he steps in a little closer. "We'd definitely be interested, Mr. McDavid."

"You get me the numbers I'm looking for on next quarter's sales report, and the suite is yours for the season."

"You've got yourself a deal," I tell him, shaking his hand even harder.

Mr. McDavid walks toward the door, calling out over his shoulder, "Ms. Jameson will be in contact."

"It was great meeting you both," she says, her bitch-brow going up as she looks at Sebastian. "Monday morning. I want to get started on this as quickly as possible."

I nod as they both walk out of the room.

"What the fuck was that?" I ask as the door shuts.

"Fuck," Sebastian says, groaning as he slouches down into one of the chairs. He leans his head back and blows out a deep breath.

As I loosen my tie, Sebastian groans again and rubs his eyes with his palms. "You've got some 'splainin' to do, Lucy," I tell him, taking the chair beside him. "She's the one, isn't she? The one from the club?" I ask, knowing I'm right before he even says it. The pieces started falling together during our pitch.

"Yes."

I lean back in my chair and laugh. Uncontrollably. I don't know why it strikes me as funny, but it does.

"It's not funny," Sebastian whines. He *literally* whines like a toddler.

Wiping the tears from my eyes, I sit up and lean over on the table as I collect myself. "Oh, but it is. This is actually the funniest turn of events I've witnessed in a long damn time."

"What the fuck am I supposed to do now?" he asks.

"You're going to do your fucking job. That's what."

The chair Sebastian was sitting in flies back as he stands up. "How in the fuck am I supposed to do that?"

I look up to see my friend coming unhinged. "It's going to be fine. You can handle this."

"Says who?" he asks, whipping around with a crazed look in his eye. "There's a reason I stopped going to that fucking club."

Wait. What?

"Wait. You stopped going to the club?"

"Yes."

"When?"

"When Kirk kicked me out for almost beating the shit out of some guy who bid on Lexie," he says loudly, pointing at the door. "That tall gorgeous blonde who has my balls in a box and carries them around in her fucking briefcase!" He kicks the chair and then sits back down in it forcefully. "How the fuck am I supposed to work with her now? I'm going to ruin this for us." He holds his head in his hands and starts pulling at his hair.

I can't watch him crumble like this, so I do the only thing a friend can do at a time like this. I walk over, put my hands on his shoulders, and force him to look at me. Then I slap him. Kind of like a girl. But it's better than me punching him in his cry-baby nose. "Wake the fuck up and get your shit together."

He looks at me with wide eyes and palms his cheek where I made contact.

"You're going to be the Sebastian Jones I know and love. You're going to kick ass and take names. You're going to be so fucking good at your job she's going to be groveling at your feet and begging to suck your dick. Got me?"

He nods, still rubbing his cheek.

"And we're going to show McDavid the best damn sales numbers he's seen, and he's going to give us that suite, and we're going to be living it up and laughing in those douchebags from Friedman's faces."

He takes a deep breath and nods again...still rubbing his cheek. *Fucking pussy.*

"You're not going to fuck this up, because I'm not going to let you." I clap his shoulder with my hand and give it a good squeeze. "Bros before hoes."

He nods again. "Yeah, okay. I can do this."

"Fuck yes, you can do this."

He stands up, and I direct him toward the door. "And we'll get that box suite."

"Yes, we will." Giving his shoulder an encouraging squeeze, I direct him out of the conference room. "But for now," I say as we walk, "we need meat and beer. Let's go get some lunch."

"Why'd you have to hit me?" he asks as he allows me to lead him down the hallway.

"It was necessary. Besides, I didn't hit you. I slapped you. It's different."

"I think you left a mark."

"Suck it up, you pussy, or I'll tell Ms. Jameson you sleep with the afghan your maw maw made for you when you were three."

"You fucking prick," he says, shaking his head as we walk down the sidewalk.

Oh, this is going to be fun.

After two half-pound burgers and a pitcher of beer, Sebastian and I are basking in our greatness. The Ms. Jameson Debacle has been put to bed for the moment, and we're discussing how we're going to make this McDavid account our bitch. The fact Mr. McDavid wants to throw in the box suite has us kicking it into high gear, wasting no time formulating a game plan. We want to be firing on all cylinders when we meet with Lexie on Monday.

Now that I know what's up, I'll be able to play referee when needed, and hopefully, we'll all three be able to work together to see this thing through. Worst-case scenario, I'll handle the meetings with Lexie solo. I'm not sure how Sebastian would handle that. Now that he's passed the shock and awe of the moment, I can tell he really likes her.

It worries me, but I feel for the guy. I try to put myself in his position, and I realize that on one hand, it sucks—having a sexual past with a client is never good—but on the other hand, it kind of feels like fate. Sebastian quit going to the club because he couldn't handle seeing Lexie with other guys. He removed himself from the situation, or rather Kirk did. And now, here she is, showing up where he least expected it.

Kind of like Quinn.

A lot like Quinn.

Just the thought of her makes me rub my chest and will my dick to mind its manners.

I wonder if she'll ever text me or if that was just her way to get rid of me.

But she agreed that we could still see each other on Sundays, even though I haven't had the chance to test that one out yet. I guess she could be planning to stand me up at the park too.

Fuck.

Sebastian excuses himself to the bathroom, and I take the opportunity to check my phone. Just in case.

Nothing.

"Refill?" the waitress asks as she walks by our table.

"Nah, just the check," I tell her, putting my phone back in my pocket and pulling out my credit card.

Part of me, the one that closely resembles a girl, wants to shoot Quinn a text. Just a *hi* or *how's your week going.* I miss her.

The waitress comes back with the check, and I hand her my card.

Just as Sebastian sits back down in the booth, I feel my pocket vibrate. I practically rip the fabric of my pants trying to get it back out, and my heart leaps out of my throat.

"What's wrong with you?" Sebastian asks, eyeing me warily.

I ignore him and look at the phone like it's grown two eyes and legs and arms...It's now my best friend in the whole wide world.

emergency

Twelve

As soon as the door to the hotel room opens, Quinn pounces.

The door slams, and I'm shoved against it while being attacked by her luscious mouth. She's everywhere all at once, and I do my best to keep up and keep my hands on her...anywhere...as long as I'm touching her.

I'd been in a meeting with my boss when I got her text this evening. It kind of came as a shock since we just met here two nights ago. Even though we don't have a set schedule, Quinn and I can usually make it a couple of days before one of us caves and sends out the bat signal. When she texted me twice within ten minutes, I dropped everything I was doing and came here as quickly as possible.

She's fucking wild tonight—ravenous—pushing me against the door, slinking down my body and kneeling in front of me.

I don't even get a chance to catch my breath or register what she's doing before she has my pants unzipped and my dick in her mouth, sucking like her life depends on it. Grabbing her hair, I twist it around my fist and thrust deeper into her mouth because I know she likes it this way.

After hooking up for the past month, I know her body and her needs as well as I know my own.

It's not always like this, though. We're not always this frantic and rough with each other. Sometimes, we fuck deep and slow, memorizing every inch of each other before coming together. Those are the nights I like best, because although we don't talk about it, and Quinn would never admit it, I can feel us growing closer.

There's something intimate and passionate about our time together.

Nights like tonight, when it's wild and primal, normally happen when one or both of us have had a shitty or stressful day and we just need to fuck it out of our systems. Quinn is obviously tenser than I am, but I'm not complaining. I'll happily screw the stress out of her anytime she needs it.

"Quinn, I'm gonna come if you don't slow down," I warn her.

She tightens her mouth around my cock but then slowly slides off, letting it pop out of her mouth, making me groan from the pleasure. When she stands, I finally take notice of what she's wearing. Or *not* wearing, to be exact. Her tits are bare, and my hands gravitate towards them, twisting and pulling her nipples. She's also not wearing panties, only a black lacy garter belt with black stockings being held on with the attached clips. Then there are the shoes—heels that make her the perfect height for me to fuck her up against the door, which is exactly what I want to do.

Quinn reaches around to my back pocket and pulls out the condom package she knows is there, tearing it open and sliding it down my length in the blink of an eye.

I slide my hand through her long hair at the nape of her neck and pull her mouth to mine, letting my tongue delve deep inside her mouth while I move my other hand between her legs. She's wet and slick and so ready for me. I can't wait another second. Turning us around, I press her back against the door. Her breaths are coming out in small pants, and a sexy smile plays on her lips. This is what she was hoping for. And I'm going to give it to her.

Kissing her jaw, I bend down and grip her knee, wrapping it around my waist. As I line up with her entrance, I lean forward and place my lips at her ear, listening as she sucks in a breath when I fill her completely.

Fuck.

"Yes," Quinn whispers, and her hot breath covers my neck before she sucks on my skin, licking and biting as I thrust harder. This is how she shows her feelings. She doesn't use words; she uses her body. She's marking my skin just as she marked my heart weeks ago, and I fucking love it. She can mark me wherever the hell she wants.

"Harder, Jude. Please."

As much as I like fucking her against the door, I need her on the bed.

I need to see her when she comes for me. Grabbing her ass, I hoist her up, carrying her to the edge of the bed and easing her down, letting my slacks drop to my feet while still inside her. Wrapping my arms around her thighs, I begin pounding into her. The blood leaves my head and goes straight to my cock, giving me a light-headed feeling, something close to euphoria.

"Fuck, yes! That's it. Just like that," she yells. I love it when she's loud, and I love that I make her that way. *Me.*

Spreading her legs, I look down at her. Her hair is wild and spread out around her head, and her hands are desperately looking for something to hold on to. One claws at the bed covers while the other grabs her breast, rolling her nipple between her finger and thumb.

So fucking sexy.

Sweat trickles down my back as my hips pivot, hitting her clit with my pelvis. When she screams for more, I drape her knees over my shoulders, getting closer...deeper...before running my thumb through her wet folds and pressing down on her clit.

Her thighs quake as she squeezes around me, and soon, her orgasm is taking over.

I love watching her let go like this. She completely embraces the full-body experience and doesn't hold back in any way. Her sounds and movements work together to express the pleasure she feels, and I wish everyone could experience sex this way.

It's beautiful.

She's beautiful.

Just before her orgasm slows, I slam into her three more times while still pressing on her swollen nub. I explode inside of her as she comes again, pulling me deeper as we ride this one out together.

Unable to stand or walk or think, I hover over her. My head is spinning, and I feel like I just ran a fucking marathon. I kiss her cheek and then her neck, slowly pulling out and immediately missing the heat and warmth.

When I think I can hold my own, I stand up and take off my remaining clothes and toss the condom into the nearby trash can. Then I crawl back onto the bed and pull Quinn to me, covering us with the blanket. Eventually, sleep takes us both, silent and sated.

Two hours later, we're awake but still lying in the same position. It took us a couple of weeks before we started wrapping ourselves around each other and allowing ourselves to sleep, and now, we do it every time. I've never been much of a snuggler, and I get the feeling Quinn wasn't either. But she's much more relaxed and talkative when we're like this, and I can't help but think we're bonding on a deeper level than just fucking.

"How's the McDavid account going?" Quinn asks as she's draped across my chest, drawing swirls on my skin with her fingertip.

"It's going well. We're pretty close to finishing the first part of the new campaign, so we'll be doing a test run soon."

"And Sebastian and Lexie?" she asks, letting out a small chuckle.

I've told Quinn all about Sebastian and Lexie and how they behaved during our pitch. Now, she expects weekly updates on them and how they pretend to hate each other while we're working on this ad campaign.

"They're as loud as ever," I answer. "They spend their time either arguing in the office or screwing in the closet, but they're getting their work done, so I don't really care. The funny thing is, they honestly think they're fooling everyone, but it's so obvious. I actually heard Lexie tell Sebastian she was bringing her flogger with her tomorrow." I groan, rubbing my eyes. The thought makes me feel like I need brain bleach.

Quinn laughs, and I love how it feels against my chest. I love everything about this moment, in fact. I wish it didn't have to end.

I run my fingers through her thick hair, and she melts deeper into me with a relaxed moan. "How's Henry doing?"

She used to tense up when I'd ask about her son, but now she simply answers my questions. "He's great." It's a small change that feels huge. "He's ready for Christmas break. I know that," she continues. "Every day, he circles something new in the toy catalog."

I chuckle, remembering how Lucy and I would spend hours circling things. Mom would always tease us and tell us we should just submit the entire catalog as our Christmas list.

She laughs. "He's obsessed with anything you can build." Her content sigh makes me do the same. And once again, I'm filled with unchecked, uncharted feelings for this woman.

I normally don't put a lot of thought into Christmas. I mean, my family always does the holiday up big, and Sebastian and I will do something fun together, but Quinn is the only person I know with a young kid. As far as I know, she only has Henry and her mom. I know she does well for herself and can provide for her family, but I want to help too. Not financially—although I totally would if she needed help—but...I want to be there for her...and for Henry.

This is where our current situation gets tricky.

Here I am, imagining being with her and Henry on Christmas Day, opening presents and having a great time, and yet, I seriously doubt she's had the same thoughts. She'll probably freak out and leave if I even suggest getting together for the holiday, so I'll just continue to bide my time...for now. That doesn't mean I won't be buying them gifts, because I absolutely will.

A smile breaks out across my face as I think about what to get Henry. It's been years since I've been to a toy store, but suddenly, I can't wait to go.

"Did you fall back asleep on me?" Quinn asks.

"No, definitely not. I was just thinking about Christmas. I bet it's fun having a kid to buy for."

She sighs, contentedly. "It is. It's kind of magical...seeing things through his eyes. Henry makes everything fun."

"I can see that. He's an awesome kid, Quinn." I lightly trace her spine with my fingertips, causing her to shiver and snuggle closer to me. "Do you get together with other family members for the holidays or do any traveling?"

She picks her head up and looks at me. "Sometimes we travel, but most of the time, it's just me, Henry, and my mom at the house. We open presents, play, and eat cookies and candy all day. I love it."

I want to ask about her dad, but she's especially beautiful right now, the way her face lights up when she talks about her family, and I don't want to ruin it or make her sad. She's never brought him up, so I can only assume he's a sore subject.

"What about you?" she asks.

"Every holiday is a big deal in the Harris family, especially Christmas. My parents go overboard on gifts for everybody—me, my sister, Lucy, and her husband, Will, and even Sebastian. Lots of food, lots of booze, and lots of laughter."

"Sounds perfect to me."

What would truly make it perfect is for her to be there with me. Henry, too. But I don't say that. Instead, I sit up, cup her face, and kiss her. As usual, the kiss escalates and soon Quinn is straddling me.

I kiss my way down her neck and across her collarbone before she pushes on my shoulders, forcing us apart.

"I have to ask you something." Her voice sounds hesitant.

"Ask me anything," I encourage her.

I rarely see Quinn look nervous or vulnerable. It makes my stomach drop with worry about what she's going to say.

"Well, I need to ask you a favor," she admits. "My hospital has this big gala every December, and I was wondering if you'd be my date." Her eyes are everywhere but on me, and her lip is firmly planted between her front teeth. The fact she's insecure about asking me to go on a date with her is ridiculous. If she only knew the things I want to do with her. It's adorable that she's unsure of my answer.

"Quinn, I'd love to go with you."

Big brown eyes fly up to meet mine, and I can't believe she's so surprised. "Really? You'll have to wear a tux. I know guys hate that kind of dress-up stuff...Well, so do I, to be honest, but...you'll really go?"

"Of course I'll go," I say, squeezing her hips for emphasis. "Just tell me when and where to pick you up, and it's a date."

"It's next week. I'm sorry I didn't ask sooner. To be honest, I wasn't sure I should ask at all."

"Why not?"

She lets out a sigh, brushing her hair back and crossing her arms over her gorgeous tits. "Because we're supposed to be fuck buddies," she says, motioning between our naked bodies, "not fuck buddies who also date."

Raising up off the bed, I pull her closer to me. "I also told you I'd be anything you need me to be, and if that means being your date for your office party, then that's what I'll be."

"Even though it's formal?" she asks, still looking so unsure of herself and this situation. It makes me want to kiss her until she forgets everything...even her name.

Instead, I assure her, "I already own a tux."

"Of course you do." She laughs, her body relaxing.

"But I do have a condition," I say, feeling her stiffen slightly.

She looks at me warily, biting back down on her lip, bracing herself for whatever my condition might be. Tit for tat and all that. "What?" she finally asks.

"You have to return the favor and be my date for my parents' Christmas party."

Her eyes grow wide and she pushes back a little. "I don't know," she says slowly. Her lip is being tortured between her teeth and the worry is firmly in place on her beautiful face. "I don't think fuck buddies should meet each other's parents." She tries to soften the blow of her words by pressing a soft hand to my chest.

"But it's okay for fuck buddies to meet co-workers and children?" I try to keep the hurt out of my voice, but I'm sure I failed. "What other rules should we establish?"

Her eyes skitter across the room before landing back on mine. "There was actually one rule I've been thinking about," she says, holding my gaze. "No being fuck buddies with anyone else." The words come quickly, like she had to rip the Band-Aid off and get them out in the open, and I inwardly smile.

"Done. No more club," I counter.

"I haven't been back since the last night I saw you there," she admits quietly.

My heart beats faster with that piece of information before leveling out. She hasn't been back. I mean, I had hoped that was the case, but I couldn't know for sure. The admission brings me so much relief I didn't even know I needed, and my body fully relaxes with Quinn in my arms.

She looks up at me, her eyes scanning my face searching for a response, but instead of saying anything, I kiss the tip of her nose.

"One more thing," she says, her voice coming out raspy. " No more getting pissy when I try to make a joke."

"What are you talking about?"

That wicked smile I love so much slips into place. "I was joking about meeting your parents."

"No, you weren't."

"Yes, I was. They sound great. I'd love to meet them."

I flip Quinn onto her back, pinning her arms above her head, causing her to laugh. Her dark hair is wild, matching the look in her eyes.

"No more making bad jokes," I add, grinding into her.

Her laughter quickly turns to moaning when my mouth travels to her neck and then down her chest, landing on her nipple. I hold both her wrists in one hand, freeing the other to attend to her other breast, just like my mouth is doing. Quinn stretches, arching her back off the bed and driving me wild. I fucking love how uninhibited she is. She loves sex, she loves to feel good, and she's not afraid to go after what she wants. I'm just glad that, for now, it's with me.

I release her hands so I can move lower, groaning as she immediately starts tugging at my hair. When I get to the apex of her thighs, I spend extra time biting and sucking on her skin until she's thoroughly marked by my mouth. She's looking at the hickey when I glance up, and her eyes are hooded and dark.

"That's so fucking hot," she says with a gasp.

"Damn right," I agree, kissing my artwork one more time before moving to her pussy and showing her just how talented my mouth is.

Thirteen

"You're fidgeting."

"Am not."

"Yes, you are," I tell the beautiful woman standing beside me in the elevator—the beautiful woman who I would like nothing more than to be taking against the wall right now. Since the second she stepped out of her car and I saw the long...long...slit up her sexy leg, I've thought of nothing but running my tongue along that bare, soft skin, directly up to the Promised Land.

"I'm nervous," she admits, watching the numbers on the elevator as they climb.

"About what?" I ask, watching her profile. Her side-swept hair looks so silky and smooth. I want to feel it, touch it...and then make a mess of it.

"You," she says in a flustered tone. "I've never brought a guy to one of these things."

"Never?" I ask incredulously.

"Never."

"Why now?" I ask as the elevator approaches the top floor.

"A few of the nurses were trying to set me up with one of the new residents. To get them off my back, I told them I already had a date. If I came without one, they would still be trying to set me up." She lets out a huff as the elevator doors open. "So, here we are."

My stomach drops a little at her confession. I mean, I didn't let myself get my hopes up that there was any more to this night than what she had said...a favor. I'm scratching her back. But the fact my being here makes her nervous and uncomfortable goes against everything inside me. The only thing I want to do is make her happy...make her feel good. I want to ease her, not make her break out in hives.

"If my being here is too stressful for you, I can fake an illness or something."

We pass a couple and Quinn greets them. I merely nod, unsure of my place.

"You'd do that?" she asks, and my stomach drops even further.

Stop being fucking Prince Charming, Harris.

Maybe Sebastian is right. Maybe I lost my balls. Or maybe I chopped them off the day I agreed to be Quinn's fuck buddy, and she now has possession of them.

"Uh, if you wanted me to. Sure."

She stops and yanks my arm, pulling me into a dark corner. "Kiss me."

"What?" I ask, wondering if she's the one who's sick. "I don't want to mess up...this," I say, waving to her gorgeous, put-together form.

Her hands grip the lapel of my tuxedo, and she pulls me to her, our mouths colliding. Her tongue forces its way into my mouth, and I happily oblige, taking her in greedily. I'm careful with the hair, but I press my body to hers, pushing her into the wall. After a minute or two, we slow down. I nip at her bottom lip, and she slides her arms up and around my neck, her lips ghosting over my cheek.

"Thank you for being here."

"You're welcome."

Pushing off the wall and looping her arm through mine, she says, "Let's go mingle."

Chuckling, I shake my head. This woman never ceases to amaze me... and keep me on my fucking toes, always guessing what she'll do or say next. "Okay," I agree, thankful she's changed her tune and all it took was kissing me in a dark corner to make that happen.

I smile and walk her toward the double doors.

The music that could be heard from the hall gets louder, and people are everywhere. Lots of sparkling dresses and men dressed in tails. A waiter walks by, offering us a glass of champagne. Quinn and I both gladly accept.

If she's feeling anything like me, she needs it. Between Quinn's nerves and our impromptu make-out session, I could actually use a shot of whiskey, but this champagne will do for now.

"Quinn," a familiar voice says, approaching from behind. My body tenses until I feel Quinn's hand on my arm.

"Cindy, you look gorgeous," Quinn says, leaning forward and placing a kiss on the cheek of the woman I've only seen one other place.

The club.

What the fuck is she doing here?"

"Jude," Quinn says. "I believe you know my friend, Cindy."

I force a smile and offer my hand. "Yes, it's nice to see you."

"So good to see you," she says with a raised eyebrow. I watch as her gaze shifts from me to Quinn and back. My being here is obviously just as much a shock to her. "Well, I was on my way to the bar. Y'all enjoy yourselves."

"You too," Quinn says as she walks off.

I down what's left in my glass as Quinn and I turn to watch the crowd.

"I guess I should've mentioned that I work with Cindy. She's a nurse in the ER," she says without looking at me. "She's who invited me to the club."

"So Cindy daylights as a nurse." I nod and let out a low chuckle. "She looked shocked as shit to see me here."

"Yeah, probably would've been good to mention you to her. Kinda slipped my mind."

"Small world."

"Yeah," she says, laughing. And I'm happy to hear it.

Looking for a distraction that's appropriate for public consumption, I glance around the room and see a dance floor with a few couples taking a spin. "We should dance."

"Oh, you dance?" she asks, looking over her shoulder at me, and I realize it's going to be damn near painful to keep myself in check tonight.

She offers me her hand and I take it, following her through the crowd. A slow song comes on, and I pull her close, loving the way she feels pressed up against me. She smells amazing. The sweet and spice I've grown accustomed to is in full force tonight, and I want to drown in it...in her.

After a couple of songs, a man steps up to the microphone and taps it. Quinn turns to the stage, and I stand to her side, placing my hand at the small of her back, needing to touch her.

Unlike a few weeks ago, she doesn't stiffen, only relaxes into my touch.

"Ladies and gentlemen, I'd like to welcome everyone to this year's Quincy Roland Holiday Gala."

The room erupts in applause, and I follow suit, clapping, but my mind is stuck on the *Quincy Roland* part. It seems there are a few things Quinn failed to mention.

"As you all know, Dr. Roland was passionate about many things, two of those being this hospital and our Cardiac Program. It was through his foundation the Cardiac Wing was built, and it's through this gala it stays open. A hospital requires generous donations from wonderful people like those of you in this room tonight. As chief of staff, I'd like to thank you for your contributions."

The band returns to playing, filling the room with a light jazz. Quinn and I both take another glass of champagne as a tray passes by and people begin to mingle again. A few stop and say, "Merry Christmas" or "it's good to see you". Quinn smiles politely, accepting hugs or kisses on the cheek. She's assuming a new role I've never witnessed before, so I stand back, giving her space and admiring how beautiful she is.

The man who was on stage a few minutes ago walks up, telling her how beautiful she looks and how proud her father would be. With that one statement, he just answered the question swirling in my mind. Quincy Roland is Quinn's dad...or *was* Quinn's dad.

"How happy would Quincy be tonight?" he asks, looking around the room.

She smiles, but there's a hint of sadness in her eyes as she scans the room and then returns to the man in front of her. "He'd be really happy."

"Have you heard the news?" the man asks.

"I don't think so," Quinn says, her eyebrows drawing together. "What news?"

"Dr. Cartwright is coming back to be head of cardio."

I watch Quinn's face morph from confused to happy...and then to something else.

Scared?

Nervous?

"Oh, really?" she asks, her voice a bit strained. It might not be noticeable to anyone else, but I see it, hear it. Over the weeks we've been meeting up, I've become so attuned to her and her body, I can't miss it. Every small nuance of Quinn Roland is charted in my mind. "I hadn't heard."

"Well, you know how these things go," the man says, cocking his head. "But as of tonight, he's slated to be back at Mercy by the new year."

"That's...great," Quinn replies, smiling up at him, but I can see something else behind that smile. I'm not sure what it is, but it's something.

"Quincy would be really happy about that too, am I right?"

I notice the way her fingers tighten around the champagne flute and I instinctively want to touch her, protect her...give her whatever she needs. "Definitely," she says with a small nod. "It's all he ever wanted."

"Well, I'll let you get back to the party." He kisses her cheek and nods to me as he walks away.

Quinn lets out a deep sigh, stiffening a little when I place my hand on her back.

What the fuck?

We are not going back to that, no way.

Bending so my lips are close to her ear, I ask quietly, "Everything okay?"

"I think I'm ready to go."

"Sure," I say, taking her empty champagne glass and setting it on another tray as it goes by. "Let's get out of here."

I want to ask so many questions, but instead, I guide her through the crowd, back down the hall and into the elevator. I let the quiet settle between us and instead of walking her to her car, since she insisted on us meeting in the parking lot, I lead her to mine. She doesn't argue nor hesitate. Once we're inside, I start up the car and head to the one place I like to go to when I'm feeling a little stressed.

Besides the Omni.

"Whataburger," Quinn says as we pull into the drive.

Looking over at her in the passenger seat, still looking so gorgeous, I take her hand and kiss her knuckles. "I'm sorry. I guess I should've asked."

"No, this is perfect." I swear there's a blush on her cheeks, but I don't comment on it.

After we get our food, we pull up into a parking spot under the streetlight and dig in.

Quinn doesn't fight me over the ketchup like Sebastian does, claiming she doesn't like ketchup on her fries because it "hides the delicious potato flavor". I think I like her more than I did five minutes ago. We'll need to go on more Whataburger dates.

Ten minutes later, we're both leaned back in our seats, and Quinn is sucking up the last drink of her float.

Guess I was wrong.

"So," I say, trying to start a conversation without freaking her out or making her upset.

"I'm sorry," she whispers, playing with the straw in her cup.

"For what?"

"I should've given you some sort of prep course. I feel like I took you in there blind. And on top of that, I've been a hot mess all night. Sometimes I don't know why you put up with me." She says that last part quietly, looking out the window.

Fighting back a smile, I admit, "You've got the hot part right."

She turns and rolls her eyes before turning her attention back to her empty cup. After a few moments, she takes a deep breath and moves in her seat to face me. "So, Quincy was my dad...*is* my dad. He died seven years ago."

"I'm sorry."

She nods sadly. "I miss him, especially on nights like tonight."

Hoping I don't make her shut down, I press for more. "How did he die?"

There's a shift in her expression and I'm afraid I hit a landmine and those walls that are so tough to tackle are on their way back up, but then she opens up. "Heart attack. How crazy is that? World-renowned heart surgeon, and he died of a heart attack."

"That's awful." My heart aches for her. I can't imagine losing my dad. And even though it's been seven years, I can still see the pain in Quinn's eyes. I'd love nothing more than to take that from her.

"He wouldn't have been able to save himself," she adds, looking back out the window. "Daniel...uh, Dr. Cartwright...He tried to save him, but it wasn't his fault either."

Things are starting to make more sense. The more I learn about her, unintentional or not, the more the puzzle pieces of Quinn Roland start to fall into place. I don't press for more and she doesn't offer anything else.

Finding out about her dad and how he died seems like enough for one night, but I have one more burning question that can't wait. While she's being so forthcoming, I ask, "Why did you go to the club? I know you said Cindy invited you, but what made you want to?" My tone leaves that question a bit open-ended. I'm hoping it comes across without judgment. I'd be the biggest hypocrite on earth if I made it anything but inquisitive.

Quinn's features hold tight and I'm afraid the wall is going to slam up in my face, but then she gives me a hint of a smile and shrugs. "I hadn't had sex in a long time. My job is demanding...but I probably have allowed it to be more so, avoiding relationships. I didn't want to introduce a man to Henry only to have them let him down. It never felt right, so I just haven't dated. When Cindy invited me, my knee-jerk reaction was no...hell no," she says, a genuine laugh following.

Swallowing, she glances down at her lap and then back up before continuing. "But the more I thought about it and the more Cindy sold it—the health records, anonymity, guarantee I'd get laid with no strings attached..." She pauses, her eyebrows going up as she inhales. "I finally agreed. The combat boots and my old car were ways for me to keep that part of my life separate, like an alias. Nights I went to the club, I wasn't Quinn Roland, daughter of Quincy Roland; or Quinn the mom; or Quinn the daughter. I wasn't even Quinn...just a woman looking to relieve some stress. And the money was easily rationalized because I haven't done anything for myself in years, hardly touching the money my father left me."

I sit back in my seat, shocked at her openness and honesty and completely afraid to say anything for fear of disturbing this place we're in.

I love how unapologetic she is. I want to tell her that, but I'm afraid even more confessions would follow, ones I'm not ready to say and she's not ready to hear.

"Thanks for telling me," I finally say. "And for what it's worth, you could've said just because and that would've been a good enough answer."

She huffs, pushing my shoulder lightly, the sadness from the talk about her father still there around the edges.

As I pull out of the parking lot, what I'd love more than anything else is to take her home with me. But I would settle for the hotel, anywhere I could make her feel better and show her what she means to me. But instead, I drive back to the parking lot where her car is parked.

When I walk around and open her door for her, she stands and kisses me deeply, with so much passion. If I let my heart come to its own conclusion, it would assume this woman considers me more than a fuck buddy. But I shut it down, reminding myself of her warning—*don't get attached.*

"Thank you for tonight and for being so understanding," she says, holding tightly to the lapels of my tux.

Kissing her forehead, I breathe her in. "You're welcome."

"I guess I'll see you Sunday," she says, sliding into her SUV.

"Yeah, I'll see you Sunday," I tell her, making sure she and her gorgeous dress are tucked safely inside before I shut her door. Once again, I stand in the parking lot and watch her taillights as she drives away.

It's only two days, but it'll be two days too long.

I miss her the second she's out of sight.

Fourteen

"I THOUGHT YOU WERE GOING TO STAND ME UP," I SAY, LEANING DOWN and kissing her nose and then her cheek.

"I might've taken the scenic route." She laughs. "But I brought wine," she says, holding up the bottle proudly.

"My mom will love you even more than she probably does already. And you wouldn't have taken the scenic route if you would've let me pick you up."

She shrugs, glancing away. "I like driving myself."

It's not a real date if I don't pick you up. That's what I want to say because I think deep down, that's her rationale. It can't be because she doesn't want Henry to see us together, because we see each other every Sunday. Maybe it's her mom. Regardless of the reasoning or the fact she drove herself, I'm glad she's here.

"Let's get inside."

I walk her up to the porch and open the door for her. My mom is there instantly, wrapping Quinn in a hug.

"It's so good to meet you," my mom says. "Jude has told us so much about you." Quinn's eyes widen over my mom's shoulder, and I can't help but laugh.

"Quinn," my dad says as my mom ushers her into the kitchen, where everyone else seems to be congregated. "I'm so glad you came."

"It's nice to meet you, Mr. Harris."

"Call me Keith, please."

"Wait a second. Like *the* Keith Harris?" she asks, her eyes widening again.

"*Sex Talk with Dr. Harris?*"

"The one and only," my dad says proudly.

My mom laughs, swatting my dad with a kitchen towel. "Don't start with that, Quinn. His ego can hardly fit through the door as it is."

Oh my God, Quinn mouths to me, and I see her cheeks flush pink.

"Hi, Quinn," my sister greets. "I'm Lucy."

The shock and awe continue as Quinn says, "You're on the show too."

"Every Tuesday and Thursday," Lucy says matter-of-factly. She and my dad's pseudo-fame doesn't go far around here. None of us allow them to get a big head over their notoriety, so seeing Quinn low key fangirl is quite entertaining.

"I...I mean, I don't listen religiously or anything," Quinn says, trying to play it cool but failing miserably. "But uh, some of the nurses are always listening in the..."

"Don't worry about it, Quinn," Will says, walking over and draping an arm over my sister's shoulders. "Everyone in this kitchen listens to *Sex Talk with Dr. Harris.* And these two were his guinea pigs," he says, laughing.

"Actually, Susan gave them the initial sex talk. She didn't trust me to stick with the basics," my dad interjects.

"He would've brought up anal on the first day," Will adds, earning an eye roll from my mother.

I watch Quinn's eyes grow exponentially and chuckle.

"And no one should bring up anal on the first day," Sebastian chimes in, reaching over the counter for a meatball.

"Can we not talk about anal in the kitchen?" my mother admonishes in her most chastising voice.

"Anal is definitely a day-two topic."

"Enough with the anal," my mom says loudly.

I look over to see Quinn hiding her laugh and a beautiful blush on her cheeks.

"Welcome to the Harrises," I whisper in her hair, pulling her to me. "Nothing says Merry Christmas like anal talk in the kitchen with your parents." She hides her face in my chest and loses it.

"Quinn," I say, trying to change the subject. "This is Will, my brother-in-law."

"How do you do?" Will says in his deep, Texas drawl.

"And this is Lexie Jameson," I say, gesturing to the tall blonde standing beside Sebastian. Apparently, they're now dating.

Lexie's well-manicured brow arches as she smiles. "Quinn, nice to see you again."

"You two know each other?" I ask, pulling back to look down at Quinn. I'd wanted to ask, but everything about *the club* is always so hush-hush.

The sly, knowing smile on her face tells me they do.

"We met once."

"At the club," Lexie adds.

"Oh, at the sex club?" my sister asks excitedly.

Quinn's big brown eyes shoot up to mine, pleading for help, but I have none to offer.

"They all know about the club. I probably should've mentioned that. Nothing is off-limits here at Casa de Harris." She jabs me in the ribs, but I can't help laughing. Turnabout is fair play. She forgot to mention good ol' Cindy, so I failed to mention my father and sister are sex therapists and talk about anal like it's the weather.

"Will and Lucy want to go there for their anniversary," Lexie says.

"Since Jude and I are pretty much black-listed, Lucy will probably be hitting you two up for a connection," Sebastian adds.

"Black-listed?" Quinn asks.

"Yeah, after Sebastian carried Lexie out of the club over his shoulder like a fucking caveman, Kirk told him never to come back."

Quinn laughs again, tilting her head back and exposing her gorgeous neck. I would love to be kissing it right now if we weren't in a room full of people. "Oh, my god. That's hysterical."

"Hey, it easily could've been Jude," Sebastian says, pointing a finger at me.

"But it wasn't. You were always so afraid I was going to get your ass kicked out, and you went and did it yourself."

"Can we not talk about this?" Sebastian pleads.

Quinn smiles as a playful, comfortable mood takes over the entire kitchen. "Oh, but it's so much fun giving you shit."

"Oh, I like her already," Lucy says.

After dinner and dessert, my dad, Will, Sebastian, and I pour ourselves a couple of fingers of Christmas Cheer, also known as Maker's Mark Black Label. We stand at the bar in my mom and dad's sitting room and watch as the girls laugh themselves silly across the room.

I love seeing Quinn like this.

I love having her here...with me.

I love everything about this night.

Admittedly, I was a little worried about my family scaring her off, but I couldn't have asked for a better night. As if she feels my eyes on her, she looks my way and smiles—a big, genuine smile—and it lights up the room more than the glow of the enormous Christmas tree.

Whether she knows it or not, she gave me my Christmas wish.

Fifteen

emergency

Shit.

I look at my phone and then back at the road.

Shit. Shit. Shit.

At the next stoplight, I text a quick reply.

30 minutes?

As I'm turning into the parking lot of the toy store, my phone buzzes from the passenger's seat again.

now

I roll my eyes and grab the phone as I climb out of the car, but I can't help the small smile that forces its way onto my face. *So impatient.*

"call 911," I type, laughing to myself before I press send. Neither of us has used that on the other since the night Quinn set the rules of our relationship. I'm not saying we haven't kept the other waiting from time to time, but eventually, we reply and show up.

Are you serious?

I'm just getting ready to reply "yes" when some lady hits me with her basket from behind.

"Son of a bi—"

"Language," the lady screeches, covering her son's ears with her hands.

"I'm sorry, but you hit me with your basket." I bend down and rub my calf where it made contact. What I want to tell her is she should watch where's she's fucking going.

Without another word, the lady turns and begins speed walking into the store, obviously on some sort of timed shopping trip or something. Maybe she's playing in one of those game shows where you only have a set amount of time to fill your basket.

My pocket vibrates, reminding me I didn't reply to Quinn's last text message.

hello?

If you'll give me 30 minutes, I'll meet you.

Fine.

What does *fine* even mean? I've never understood that. Does it mean *okay, I'll see you in 30* or *forget it, you loser, I'll find someone else to bang?*

I don't text back. I decide to leave it at that. Maybe I'll pick her up some flowers on the way to soften her up a little. Although, I'm not sure if she even likes flowers. I should know that. That's an important thing to know about the woman you're...fucking.

Sometimes, I have to remind myself that's all we are—fuck buddies. We still haven't made any changes to our arrangement...no official declarations of dating status.

I admit I allow the lines to blur, occasionally, but only in my head.

Once inside the store, I grab a basket and set off on a mission to find the coolest toy possible. I didn't ask Quinn's permission to do this. Maybe I should have, but I kind of feel like mine and Henry's relationship is its own thing. We've bonded over our Sundays in the park and our love for Fergie. I also found out last week that he's obsessed with Star Wars. When I was looking around online for something cool to buy him, I found this four-foot-tall Stormtrooper that makes all kinds of cool sounds. I thought it might be something he doesn't have and possibly something Quinn wouldn't buy.

Standing in the middle of the cluttered store, I realize I don't have the first clue where to find it. It's been a good fifteen years since I've stepped foot into a toy store. I try to find a person who looks like they work here but come up empty-handed. After a few minutes pass, I decide I can't just stand around wasting time, so I start walking—up and down every aisle—looking for something Star Wars. Surely, they keep all of that stuff together.

On the fourth aisle, my phone buzzes again.

room 1913

When I check the time, I realize it's already been fifteen minutes.

Shit.

Picking up the speed, I start zig-zagging the aisles again.

Bingo!

After scanning over half the store, I turn down one of the aisles and see the prize on the top shelf and there's only one. Looks like it's my lucky day.

If I hurry, I can snag the Stormtrooper and be at the hotel room with a minute or two to spare.

Reaching up to grab it off the shelf, my phone buzzes again and I groan, rolling my eyes at Quinn's persistence today. I actually love that about her, but she's really imposing on my toy shopping.

I'm about to text her back that I'll be there soon when a blur of activity takes place in front of me.

A woman climbs on the bottom shelf, reaches up, and snags the Stormtrooper, placing it in her cart. Right in front of me.

"That's mine," I tell her, because it is. I'm standing right in front of it and was just getting ready to take it off the shelf and put it into my own shopping cart before Quinn's text side-tracked me.

"Um, no. It's in my basket, therefore, it's mine." The arch of her eyebrows tells me she means business, but I'm ready to fight for this. I drove all the way across town to this particular toy store because when I looked online they said it was in stock. I need this Stormtrooper. Without it, I'll be back at square one, trying to come up with the perfect gift for Henry...and *this* is the perfect gift for Henry. So, I need this fucking Stormtrooper.

"Actually," I begin, trying to stay calm. "I was just getting ready to put it in *my* basket before you came around the corner and swiped it."

"I didn't *swipe* it," she says, annoyance thick in her voice. "It's free game as long as it's on the shelf." The way she rolls her eyes, like this is information I should know, pisses me the hell off.

"Well, it was rude of you to swoop in and grab it right out from under me."

"Guess you shoulda been faster," she challenges, pushing my cart out of the way with hers and walking past me.

I can't let her get away.

I need that Stormtrooper.

It's two days before Christmas.

I don't have time to keep looking.

"Ma'am," I call out to her retreating form, but she doesn't turn around.

I abandon my empty cart in the aisle and walk quickly to catch up with her.

"Ma'am!"

"This is harassment," she says, whipping her blonde hair around. "Do I need to get a manager?"

I huff, completely put out by the turn of events. "Good luck finding one of those."

"Go. Find. Something else. To buy." Her eyes are wild and unhinged and I almost give up.

Almost.

"I need *that*," I say, pointing into her basket.

"Yeah, well, it's the last thing I need on my kid's Christmas list, so you're not getting this one."

She continues walking up toward the checkout line and I start to panic.

My phone buzzes again and I want to throw it across the store. Quinn really needs to chill. She has no idea what I'm dealing with here.

I'll be there, I text back, wanting to add a bunch of exclamation points after it to show my annoyance.

Are you in a meeting?

Oh, my God. What is with the questions? I don't reply because Blondie is getting away with my Stormtrooper. As I watch her hand over her debit card, I decide I'll let her pay out and give myself a minute to calm down and gather my wits. I can do this. If I can land big advertising accounts, I can convince a woman to give up a Stormtrooper.

Money talks, right?

Walking out the exit, I wait.

When she walks out a few minutes later, I approach with my hands raised in surrender, trying to make her feel comfortable. The last thing I need is for her to call the cops or something.

"So, your kid really wants that Stormtrooper, huh?" I begin, still trying to think of the right thing to say.

She groans in frustration and rolls her eyes as she pushes her cart past me and toward her car.

"I get it. I mean, I don't have kids or anything, but—"

"Are you kidding me?" she says, turning around. "Are you one of those weird fanboys or something?"

I frown, not knowing what she's talking about, but then I realize she thinks I want it for myself. "No," I say, running my hand through my hair and deciding on the straight forward approach. "My uh...girlfriend's little boy...I'm buying it for him. This is the first time I've bought him a gift and I want it to be something cool...something he'll remember." Quinn would probably kill me for calling her my girlfriend, but I can't call her my fuck buddy in front of a stranger, besides that wouldn't convey my feelings for Henry.

"So, you're trying to make a good impression...win the kid over. Trying to get in his mom's pants, I'm sure," she hisses, crossing her arms over her chest and tapping her foot like she has me pegged.

I laugh and scrub my hand down my face. *If she only knew.* "It's not like that. I'm not trying to buy his affection. We hang out and stuff. I think he already likes me." *Why the fuck am I spilling my guts in the toy store parking lot?* "I just want to buy him something he'll like. I've never had the chance to buy for a kid on Christmas," I admit, ready to give up.

She must sense my desperation, because her face softens, and I think I might detect a teeny tiny smile. So, I go in for the kill.

"I'll pay you double what you just bought it for. That should buy your kid something really nice."

The eyebrows go up again, but this time it's in consideration of my offer.

A few seconds pass and she glances back to the basket, before meeting my eyes. "Deal."

I smile in triumph and pull out my wallet.

As me and my, I mean, *Henry's* Stormtrooper are driving down the highway, headed to the Omni, my phone buzzes again. I glance over and see the message pop up on my screen.

Are you seriously going to stand me up?

On my way.

I might be gone when you get here.

Bullshit.

Five minutes later, I'm in the elevator on my way to the 19th floor with the biggest grin on my face, because I feel like I won the McDavid account all over again. Who knew bargaining in a parking lot over a Stormtrooper could feel so rewarding?

Knocking on the door, I wait for Quinn to open it. She takes her sweet ass time, but I know she's still in there. It might be my imagination, but I think I catch a whiff of her sweet and spicy scent. My mind begins to run wild and my cock stirs to attention. I haven't had much time to think about her and what I'd like to do to her, seeing as I've been a bit preoccupied. But now that I'm standing here in front of this door, knowing she's on the other side, I need her.

Knocking once more, I lean my ear to the door. "Housekeeping," I say in a high-pitched voice. "Want me to fluff your pillows?"

Quinn finally opens the door and smiles, shaking her head, before grabbing me by the shirt and pulling me inside.

"I'll fluff your pillow," she growls before kissing me roughly. Her teeth graze my lip and I love the sting, the intensity. I kiss her back hard and press her against the door.

"What was so fucking important?" she asks with one hand in my hair and one gripping my cock through my pants.

"A toy," I tell her, grinding against her.

"What kind of toy?" she asks, insinuation thick in her tone, but all I can think about is what I want to do with *my* toy.

"Aren't we Little Miss Nosy." I laugh, loving this shift where Quinn is the one seeking information and needing me. Picking her up, I carry her to the bed. After I devour her mouth, I feast on the rest of her, taking my time and doing everything right...making sure she knows how much I want her.

Sixteen

"Ten!"

"Nine!"

"Eight!"

I grab Quinn's waist and pull her body against mine. "Pucker up, buttercup. It's almost midnight." That didn't sound nearly as suave out loud as it did in my head, but in my defense, I've had a few beers. And a couple of shots of tequila. Thank goodness Quinn is laughing at me and not pushing me away.

Quinn and I originally made plans to meet at the hotel tonight, but when Sebastian invited us both to celebrate the New Year at the bar with him and Lexie, I took a chance and asked her.

To my surprise, she agreed, and here we are.

Tightening my grip on her hips, I zero in on Quinn's full lips. Her tongue peeks out, wetting her bottom lip and causing my dick to harden. I can't wait to get to the hotel so we can spend the entire night together.

"Three!"

"Two!"

"One!"

It's as if a gun has gone off, signaling the beginning of a race as our mouths collide, making us both winners. All of the cheering, noise-makers, and music fade into the background, and it feels like Quinn and I are the only two people in the room...the whole fucking world. There's something different about this kiss—it's fierce, passionate, promising—and I hope with everything in my soul that she feels it, too.

"Let's get out of here," Quinn whispers.

Moving faster than I ever have in my life, I drop a few bills on the bar to pay our tab, then grab her hand and head for the door while waving at Sebastian, letting him know we're leaving.

The cold air that surrounds us as soon as we're outside is a refreshing change from how it felt in the crowded bar, but I make sure to keep my arm around Quinn, holding her close to keep her warm.

"I'll drive," she says as she presses in closer, hiding her face in my jacket from the cold January wind.

"Are you sure?"

"Yeah, I only had a couple of beers. I'm fine. I'll drop you back at your car later."

"Okay." I don't argue because I've definitely had more to drink than she has, and I don't want to waste time or be away from her.

I can't stop touching her, even in the car. I lean over the console and nip at her neck and ear, teasing the soft skin just under her shirt.

"Stop, you're driving me crazy." Quinn's hands stay firmly on the steering wheel, but I can see her eyes flutter closed and then back open. Driving a little faster, she makes no effort to push me away, so I know her complaints are invalid.

She wants me just as much as I want her.

I'd take her here if she'd let me.

I'd take her anywhere, anytime, any way she'd let me.

I don't see that ever changing.

Unable to stop myself, I lick and suck at her neck, and I'm rewarded when her entire body shivers in response. She tastes so good. I didn't know skin could taste so sweet, so perfect. "We could just go to my apartment. It's not far from here," I tell her, my lips against her neck. This time, instead of a shiver, she stills and then shifts away from me, pulling her head back.

"We can't do that."

Sitting back in the seat, I watch her in the pale glow of the interior lights of her SUV. Her eyes stay trained on the road, but I can tell by the way she works her bottom lip with her teeth that something's on her mind.

"I don't get what the big deal is," I say breaking the silence. The liquid courage still coursing through my system making me brave.

"It's not part of the agreement."

"I thought maybe we could get past the agreement. I mean—"

"Can we not do this tonight?" she cuts me off with a level of pleading and need to her voice I haven't heard outside the bedroom...hotel room, excuse me.

"Fine."

We continue through the next stoplight and pull into the drive of the hotel. Neither of us speaks as we get out of the vehicle and allow the valet to park it. I walk up to the desk and request a room, and after a quick transaction, I take Quinn's hand and walk towards the elevator.

On the way up, I think about making her talk and refusing to go through with this if she won't tell me what's going on. I want to force her to tell me why we can be seen together in public and attend parties together, but she won't even entertain the thought of coming to my apartment. I want to say something, but I can't.

Maybe I'm weak.

Maybe I want her too bad.

Maybe I'm scared she'll call the whole thing off.

So instead of talking, I hold her hand, rubbing my thumb over hers.

When the elevator stops on the tenth floor, I walk silently down the hall and open the door, leading Quinn inside. No words are exchanged as we undress each other. It's not hurried or needy like earlier. It's not hard and desperate like we sometimes are. It's slow and deliberate with our eyes locked on each other.

Small moans of pleasure and pleas of want fill the quiet room.

The only light filling the room is from the open window and the city surrounding us. Quinn's creamy skin blends into the white comforter with her dark hair a stark contrast.

"You're so beautiful. I could look at you like this forever," I whisper, running my hand between her breasts and down her stomach, slipping a finger under the small silky piece of fabric. Ridding her of that last stitch of clothing, I lean down and begin to kiss all the skin I've wanted to all night but couldn't, taking my time and telling her how I feel with my actions, hoping they'll suffice for now.

When I make my way to her sweet pussy, spreading her legs, I glance up to see her eyes closed.

"Open your eyes, Quinn. Watch what I do to you."

She obeys, slowly opening her eyes, letting me see the emotions she was hiding. Her hands latch onto my hair as I lick up her slit, pushing my tongue farther in, tasting her, relishing in her—being consumed by Quinn.

Her taste.

Her smell.

Her touch.

The combination is lethal. It's enough to make me come and could very well be the end of me.

When I slip two fingers inside her, Quinn begins to writhe under me, her hips seeking what she desires...taking what she needs.

The faster I pump, the more she loses control.

Her hands leave my hair and grab frantically at the blanket beneath her.

Her body begins to tremble.

Her mouth falls open with silent cries of ecstasy.

Her walls tighten around my fingers, and I want it to be my cock.

Without hesitation, I climb up her body and wrap my arms around her thighs, pulling her to where I need her. As she's still riding out her orgasm, I thrust inside, forcing out a loud cry of pleasure.

Quinn's eyes fly open and find mine. The sweat on her brow shines as her look of desire grows. Her gaze goes from my face to where we're joined, and she watches as I thrust in and out.

"Oh, God. So good."

"So fucking good, Quinn."

I begin pressing down on her clit, coaxing out another orgasm from her, taking her to the edge and helping her fall.

I love watching her completely lose control and knowing I'm responsible for it.

I love watching her like this...vulnerable, exposed...so much different than how she normally is.

As she closes in around me, her thighs squeezing tightly on my torso, I lose control myself—heart beating wildly, sweat pouring, erratic thrusts.

And then oblivion, where the only thing that exists is us.

Moments pass as we try to regain our breaths. My muscles are so spent I can barely hold myself up.

"Every time," she says breathlessly. "Every time, I think it's the best yet, but then the next time, I'm proven wrong. Somehow, each time is better than the last."

I lean down and kiss her damp forehead. "I agree." I roll lazily off her and sprawl out beside her on the bed, letting the world spin around us.

After I catch my breath, I rid myself of the condom and crawl up beside Quinn. Now would probably be a good time to have that talk, but I can't force myself to ruin the moment. Instead, I pull her to me and bury my face in her hair, inhaling deeply and wishing we could stay like this forever.

Seventeen

I'M NOT SURE WHO'S MORE EXCITED FOR OUR SUNDAY AFTERNOON IN the park, me or Fergie. Quinn and I agreed to skip our usual park date on the Sunday after Christmas, so it's been two weeks since we've all been together. Of course, I'm happy to see Quinn again, but I'm really excited to see Henry because I can finally give him the gift I bought him.

I admit, it's pretty damn cool. I had to wrap the enormous box so I'd stop playing with it. There's a slim chance it might already need some new batteries, so I bought those too.

Fergie starts running in small circles, barking excitedly to let me know she spots Quinn and Henry. Less than a minute later, Henry is on his knees in front of my dog, petting behind her ears and telling her how much he missed her. When I look up, I watch Quinn slowly walk toward our bench with a tight smile on her face.

Something's wrong. I know it. I've sensed it since New Year's Eve and her shutting me down when I suggested we go to my apartment, but she won't talk to me about it. I hate seeing her struggle. It's in a man's nature to want to fix things and make everything better, but Quinn is too stubborn and independent to let me help. They're qualities I both admire and find insanely frustrating.

She sits next to me and seems to relax a fraction, especially when she sees how happy Henry and Fergie are together. It's impossible to not be happy when those two are around.

"They sure are quite the pair, aren't they?" she says, finally speaking.

"They are," I agree, wondering if now is a good time to give Henry the gift. I've hesitated for the past couple weeks, unsure if it would be a good move or a bad one. Lately, I seem to be walking on eggshells where Quinn is concerned. "Hey, I have that gift for Henry. Do you mind if I give it to him?"

Quinn genuinely smiles and says, "Not at all."

Maybe I've been worried for nothing?

"Henry, come here for a minute. I have something for you."

He looks my way, and when he sees the large and horribly wrapped gift beside me, he rushes over.

"This is for me?" he asks, eyes wide.

"It sure is. I saw it and knew you had to have it. Open it up, buddy."

Thankfully, he doesn't seem to care about how badly I wrapped his present because he wastes no time in ripping the shiny paper to shreds, revealing the Stormtrooper. Not knowing any other kids very well, I had no idea how fun it is to watch one open a gift. I could do this all day. The look of awe and joy on his face makes the extra money I gave that lady at the toy store totally worth it.

I would've paid even more just for this moment.

"Mom, look! It's the Stormtrooper I wanted!" He holds up the box that's almost as big as he is to show her, as if there was a chance she missed seeing it.

"That's awesome, Henry! What do you say to Jude?"

"Thank you, Jude. Thank you so much!" He rushes to me and gives me a quick hug, and fuck, if it doesn't feel amazing. "I'm gonna leave it here while Fergie and I play. I don't want her to think it's her toy."

Quinn and I both laugh as Henry and Fergie run off with a frisbee. I have the biggest smile on my face and when I turn to Quinn, the same one is on hers. It's genuine, and it makes me relax.

"Where did you find that?" she questions. "I looked all over the city and online and couldn't get one."

Not wanting her to know exactly how I was able to purchase the toy, I tell her, "It's all in who you know."

She side-eyes me before thanking me. "You've made his day."

"No, I'm pretty sure he's made mine. I mean, I hoped that he'd like it, but I had no idea he'd react like that. He's such a great kid, Quinn."

"He is." Now her smile isn't reaching her eyes, and her shoulders are slumped. I can't take it anymore, the mood shifting once again.

"What's going on?" I ask, exhaling, hating that we have to have this talk, but damn it, I have to know what's wrong. "Please tell me what's wrong."

Quinn leans back against the bench but keeps her eyes trained on where Henry and Fergie are running and playing. "I didn't want to have this talk here, but..."

Her eyebrows furrow, and her teeth bite down on her lip. The struggle is so evident on her face, but I don't know what she's fighting. If she'd tell me, I'd gladly fight it for her...dragons, fire, the grocery store on Sunday. I'd do anything for her, if she'd just let me.

"Remember at the party when Dr. Wilson mentioned that Dr. Cartwright was coming back?" she asks, rubbing nervous hands down the front of her jeans before leaning forward on her elbows, allowing her head to sag, her hair creating a curtain around her face.

"I remember. He's the guy who tried to save your dad," I recall her story from the Whataburger parking lot.

"Yeah, he was my dad's protégé, for lack of a better word. If my dad could've adopted him, he would have." She laughs, but there's not a lot of humor behind it. "I guess he saw himself in Daniel and took him under his wing, teaching him everything he knew."

"So, were the two of you close?" I know there's a lot she's not telling me. I can feel it, but I'm not going to let her put her walls up and keep me out this time. "You and Daniel?" I clarify.

"Not really. When he first came to Mercy, I was still in school. But after I got hired on in the ER, I got to know him. Like I said, he and my dad were close. He would come over for family dinners and stuff like that. All of his family is up north, so my parents took it upon themselves to make him feel at home and be his surrogate family."

"Are you happy he's coming back?" I ask, prodding for more information.

She lets out a deep breath and sits back up, leaning back on the bench and folding her arms tightly around her torso. "It's so complicated."

"What's complicated?"

She growls out in frustration and scrubs her face with her hands. "I don't want to have this conversation."

Leaning forward, I take her hands from her face and force her to look at me. "Just say whatever you need to say. Rip it off like a Band-Aid." As much as I don't want to hear whatever it is, she needs to tell me because I hate seeing her like this. "There's nothing you can say that'll make me feel any differently about you."

"I wouldn't be so sure about that."

"Try me."

She closes her eyes and begins. "After my dad died, Daniel was as lost as I was. He was the man we both depended on, and without him here, we were both drifting...trying to find our way...trying to figure out how to go on without him. His death left a big hole everywhere—the hospital, home...life. After a few weeks, Daniel came over for dinner. My mom insisted that we all continue to do the things my father would've wanted, which included family dinners. She said that's the way we would keep his memory alive, by *carrying on*." Quinn pauses, looking out to where Henry is, watching him. Her voice is a little shaky, so I rub the backs of her hands, encouraging her to continue.

"Eventually, things at the hospital started to go back to normal, and Daniel and I spent more and more time together. Without my dad there as a middle man, the two of us started leaning on each other. Any time I would miss my dad or wish he was there for me to ask a question or something like that, I'd turn to Daniel. Anytime Daniel was feeling lonely or needed a friend, he'd come find me. We'd sneak down empty corridors to talk, but after a while, the talks turned into more. I can't really say when my feelings toward him turned romantic, but I guess somewhere between heartache and healing, they did." She pauses and dread seeps into my bones.

"We talked about moving in together, but I didn't want to leave my mom by herself. Daniel understood and never pressured me into anything. One day, Daniel said he'd been offered a job at a hospital up north—head of cardiac, exactly what my dad had been molding him for. And two weeks later, he left."

We sit there quietly. Pieces of the puzzle start falling into place, but my heart doesn't allow my head to jump to conclusions. I need to hear it from her.

"I found out I was pregnant with Henry a week after Daniel left."

She swallows hard and looks down at where our hands are laced together. "I wanted to tell him, but it never seemed like the right time. After a few weeks, he stopped calling. Somewhere deep inside, I felt like I was doing the right thing by letting him go. The hospital needed him. This was what he'd worked so hard for. Telling him about Henry seemed like a bad idea."

Her gaze turns back to the little boy, and I can't imagine why she would think telling Daniel about Henry would ever be a bad idea. He's such an amazing kid. Anybody would be lucky to be his dad. "If Daniel wouldn't have wanted him, it would've killed me. If Daniel would've wanted him and left the position to move back here, I would've felt guilty. I was still mourning the loss of my father. I couldn't mourn the loss of Daniel. I had a baby to think about."

"What did your mom say?"

"She wanted me to tell him, but she let me do what I thought was best."

I nod, trying to process the information I've been given and wondering what this means for us, but I'm too afraid to ask.

"She's been wonderful. I don't know what I would have done without her. But she says Henry saved her. He gave her something to focus on when all she wanted to do was crawl in bed and never come out. She's always been a devoted mother and now an even more devoted grandmother. She'd do anything for him."

I can tell Quinn is still avoiding something. She starts shifting on the bench and biting her lip.

"What does all of this mean?" I finally ask.

"Daniel will be back on Tuesday."

"For good?"

She shrugs, looking a little lost and confused and I hate every second of it. "I guess. He's taking over my dad's position at the hospital."

"And?"

"I'm going to have to tell him about Henry...I *want* to tell him about Henry."

I nod, agreeing. "That's good. I think you should." I let myself take a breath and ease back a little. Maybe that's all this is. She just needed to get this off her chest.

"All I've ever wanted was a family for Henry...a real family, with a mom and dad, living in the same house. I want what I had...family dinners and game nights. I've always dreamed that Daniel would come back, and when he found out about Henry, he'd want all of that too."

And there it is—the shoe I've felt hanging in the air, waiting to drop for the last couple of weeks.

Thud.

When I look up and meet her eyes, there are unshed tears in them.

"I don't want to have regrets, Jude," she pleads, begging for my understanding. "I feel like giving Daniel a chance is what's right. It would make my dad happy."

"Will it make you happy?" The bit of anger and a whole lot of frustration bites through my words. "Is that what *you* want or what you think your dad would want?"

Quinn's back stiffens and she sits up straighter. "It's what *I* want. It's what's best for Henry. He's my top priority. I have to give this a chance."

I turn to look at Henry and Fergie. Henry looks our way and smiles a big toothy grin. He deserves to be happy. He deserves everything Quinn was talking about. I'd be a horrible human being if I tried to keep him from that.

"Okay, then," I concede, trying not to sound as broken as I feel.

"He's going to miss this," she says sadly.

I swallow down the lump in my throat, refusing to show her any more of myself than I already have. "I'm going to miss this," I admit, unable to stop the words from coming out of my mouth. Right behind them are things like *I love you...choose me...let me make you happy.* But I swallow those down as well.

"Thank you," she whispers, wiping at her cheek. "For everything."

I want to reply, but my words and emotions are caught in my throat.

I want to tell her so many things, but I don't because we agreed...don't get attached.

Leaning forward, I place a kiss on Quinn's temple, breathing her in one last time.

"Be happy, Quinn. Let yourself love."

She hiccups a sob, and I can't stick around to watch it. My resolve will crumble at her feet.

"Fergie," I yell, calling her over. She and her partner-in-crime come running. When they get to the bench, I ruffle Henry's hair and tilt his head up to look at me. "Take care of your mom, okay?"

"Okay," he says, a hint of confusion in his big brown eyes.

"Fergie, tell Henry bye."

The two of them kiss on each other, and I want to scoop Henry up into a big hug, but I don't.

I can't.

"Bye, Quinn."

She gives me a sad smile and waves, pulling Henry to her.

This time, it's her watching *me* leave, but it doesn't feel any better.

My heart still wants her.

Eighteen

"ARE YOU GOING TO WORK ALL NIGHT AGAIN?" SEBASTIAN ASKS, standing in the doorway of my office.

"I don't know. Maybe."

I stretch back in my chair, staring at the blank blue screen. I'm not actually working on anything at the moment, but he doesn't need to know that.

"You should call it a night, bro. Too much work makes Jude grumpy."

"I'm fine." I yawn and stretch. "I'll probably take a break and go get some coffee or something." I assure him, just wanting him to leave already.

He finally lets out a long sigh and puts his coat on. "Whatever you say. Don't forget we have that meeting with Mr. Jones in the morning. I hope you're not wearing the same thing you are now."

"What's wrong with what I'm wearing?" I ask, looking down at my shirt. It's not dirty.

"Nothing, other than that was what you were wearing yesterday."

I roll my eyes and pick up a piece of paper to wad up and throw at him, but he ducks out before I can. He's right. I slept here last night. My sister went to my apartment and picked up Fergie for me, letting her run around in her backyard and sleep over. I'm sure she wouldn't mind doing that for me again tonight.

Looking out the window at the city below, I let my eyes travel across the tops of the buildings to one in particular. Before, it was like a beacon in the night, but now, it's a thorn in my side, reminding me of everything I've lost.

I try to not go there, even in my mind, but it betrays me.

Even when I try to think of anything but her, I still somehow end up thinking of her. Everything reminds me of her—a text message, a random Monday night, a random Tuesday night, having a drink, eating a burger. It feels like there's nothing I can do to escape her memory.

But maybe I'm not trying hard enough.

Then again, maybe I don't want to.

It's only been three weeks, but they've been the worst three weeks of my life. I don't know how I let myself fall so hard for her. She never promised me anything. We only had an agreement, and that agreement had nothing to do with commitment or love, but by God, I felt both...committed and in love. Maybe I should've told her. That thought crosses my mind about a hundred times a day. What if? What if I would've asked her to stay with me? What if I would've told her how I felt...feel? What if I would've said no?

No, Quinn. You can't try with Daniel. He'll never love you like I do. He'll never love Henry like I do.

I laugh harshly at myself and the stupidity that runs through my mind.

There's no way I would've done that. The crazy thing is that I love her so much I'm willing to let her go. I can't begrudge the fact she wants to give Henry a family. He deserves one. And I can't hold it against Quinn for wanting to try to make up for past mistakes. I actually admire her for being willing to be honest and upfront with me, for finally opening up. She could've kept fucking me while seeing if things with Daniel worked out. I probably would've never known. But she didn't. And I'm still trying to get over the goodbye.

I'm sure I will, in time.

It's not like she left me at the altar or anything. She didn't cheat on me. She didn't tell me she loved me and then took it back. She didn't tell me I could love her. I did that all on my own. So if there's anyone to blame for this heartache I can't seem to get rid of, it's me.

Just as I'm getting ready to make a call to Lucy, my phone rings, and I jump.

Every fucking time.

My stupid fucking heart must still think there's a chance or some shit, because it never fails that if my phone makes the slightest noise, I jump and look at it like it's going to solve the world's problems or at least ease the pain and emptiness in my chest.

"Hi, Lucy," I say, exhaustion evident in my raspy tone.

"Your dog misses you."

I grimace, thankful she can't see me. I know this isn't Fergie's fault, but when I look at her, all I see is Henry, which leads directly to Quinn. To me, they are a package deal.

"I have to work late," I tell her, lying through my teeth. There is nothing pressing on the desk in front of me. Actually, I'm so caught up, I'm doing the slacker-ass intern's work.

Lucy lets out a sad sigh. "Okay," she says, pausing a minute before continuing. "Will you be home tomorrow night? It's Friday."

It's a good thing she told me, because I honestly wasn't sure what day today was.

"Uh, yeah."

"Okay, I'll drop Fergie off around seven. Will and I have dinner reservations at this new place downtown at seven thirty."

"Okay. And thanks for keeping her, Lucy."

"You're welcome."

We both sit in silence, neither of us saying goodbye. Maybe she's waiting for me to hang up. Maybe I'm doing the same. Regardless, the phone is quiet, and I stare out the window again, letting my brain drift away.

"You can't keep doing this."

"I know."

"Mom won't let you miss another Sunday dinner."

"I know."

"I love you."

"Love you too, Luce."

The phone goes quiet again, but this time it's because Lucy hung up. I finally do the same and then loosen my tie. Looking around my office, I realize I am actually tired. Maybe I'll go catch a few hours of sleep on Sebastian's couch in his office.

I walk down the dark hallway, stopping by the break room and peeking through everyone's takeout boxes of leftovers. There's one marked "DM" in black marker. I crack the box and take a whiff. When the contents of the box register with my empty stomach, it growls audibly, begging for the beef fajitas inside. I can't remember the last time I had a full meal. I've been living off of Hot Pockets and granola bars.

Popping the box in the microwave, I decide DM won't mind. DM can suck it if he does. I've been doing DM's work for the last fucking week. He owes me this much.

When the microwave shuts off, I pull out the hot fajitas, grab a fork, and go to Sebastian's office.

There on the couch is a folded-up blanket and a pillow.

He must've brought it from home.

I don't know why, but the gesture hits me right in the gut.

I pull my phone out of my pocket with my free hand and open up my text messages.

Thanks for the pillow and blanket.

You're welcome. It was Lexie's idea.

You told Lexie I'm sleeping at the office?

Stop sleeping at the fucking office and you won't have to worry about it.

I roll my eyes and pocket my phone, falling onto the plush couch. Damn, I should've gotten one of these instead of a fucking pool table.

Nineteen

"Have you tried talking to her?" Sebastian asks from the other side of the small table at the café down the street from our office.

I take another drink from my coffee and continue to watch people walk past the large window, trying to avoid Sebastian's nosy-ass questions. "No."

"Don't you think it might be a good idea? I mean, you can't continue to mope around all the time. It's not good for you, and it's not good for business. Do you know Mr. Jones told Mr. Wallace that he thinks you're depressed?"

Snapping my head toward Sebastian, I frown. "What?"

"Yeah, he said his wife is a psychologist and you're a textbook example of someone dealing with depression."

"How the fuck would he know?"

"Oh, I don't know. Maybe because the two of you have been working side by side on this new account for the past two weeks."

Sitting up straighter in an effort to defend myself, I protest. "I've been nothing but professional."

"And withdrawn," he retorts. "You hardly eat. You barely sleep. And I'm not the only one who notices that you wear the same shirt and tie for days in a row."

"I do my fucking job," I say through gritted teeth, leaning forward on the table. I don't need anyone telling me what's going on in my fucking head. My head is fine. I sit back in my chair and direct my gaze back out the window, muttering to myself, "I do my fucking job."

"We all know you do your fucking job, but that's about all you do these days."

"None of the rest of it is anybody else's business."

This time it's Sebastian who snaps. "It's mine. I'm your best friend, man." His voice increases in volume, drawing the attention from a few patrons. "I'm not going to sit around and watch you be miserable over some chick. I've never seen you like this. You've gotta snap out of it and get a grip. Go on a date. Get laid. But for the love of God, quit with this heartbroken Romeo and Juliet bullshit."

"Romeo and Juliet died," I say blankly.

He leans forward on the table. "Well, sometimes I think I need to check your pulse."

"Shut the fuck up."

"Make me."

The two of us sit there, stewing in our own annoyance with each other.

"You should talk to her," Sebastian finally says after a while. "I think that's what has you so twisted up. You didn't get to tell her how you feel."

Just the mention of talking to Quinn has my insides twisted up. "And what then? Huh?"

"At least she'll know, and you won't have all these fucking regrets."

"And what if she's happy?" I ask putting all my fears on the table.

Sebastian sits back, staring across the table with an unreadable expression. "She'll tell you it was nice knowing you, and that's that."

"I'm not going to complicate matters and make things harder for her. You didn't see how upset she was. It'd be a dick move," I tell him, my mind pulling up a vivid picture of a distraught Quinn. "I can't do that to her."

Sebastian's frustration grows and then morphs into something else entirely. "What if she's not happy? What if she realizes the error of her ways and wants you back but she's afraid she's ruined everything?"

"I don't know."

He watches me for a second and I avert my gaze out the window, feeling the pressure of his scrutiny. "Does that scare you?" he asks, getting to the bottom of it. "Is that what you're afraid of?"

When I don't respond, he pushes further. "And you love her?"

"Yes," I admit, because why the fuck not. This is Sebastian after all, and he won't stop until he has all the facts.

"Still?" he asks, prodding.

Exhaling, I run a hand through my already messed up hair. "Yes. Probably more than I did before...all of that absence makes the heart grow fonder shit has some validity to it."

"Well, then you owe it to her and yourself to get your head out of your ass and go talk to her."

Unable to admit that what he's saying feels right. I should go talk to her. I want to. But I'm afraid of everything—what seeing her might do to me, what she might say, what she won't say...everything. "What the fuck ever," I mumble, partially to him and partially to myself.

"You know I'm right."

I shake my head, refusing to tell Sebastian he's right.

He's the last person on earth who needs his ego stroked.

Sitting in my car, warming my hands with a cup of somewhat hot coffee, I feel like an undercover cop. You know those movies where the cops sit out in front of a criminal's house or place of work, waiting to catch them in the act? Like that.

Basically, I'm on a stake-out.

Actually, it's more like I'm a fucking stalker, at least that's how I feel.

Ever since my talk with Sebastian a couple of days ago, all I can think about is talking to Quinn. I thought about texting her, but I couldn't bring myself to send it. I thought about giving her a call, but I wasn't sure if she'd answer.

So here I am, camped out in front of the hospital like a fucking weirdo. I'm surprised security hasn't come over and told me to leave.

I guess this is public property. I mean, I've seen all types of people come and go since I've been here. Some people are sick. Some people are visiting sick people. Some people are taking care of the sick people. There's actually another lady sitting in her car on the opposite side of the lot. She's been there for a while. From what I can tell, she's reading a book, probably taking a break from whatever she's at the hospital for.

As I'm making up a scenario for the woman reading in her car, I see a black SUV pull into the parking lot that I know to be staff parking. I sit up straighter in my seat and put my coffee in the cupholder.

My heart beats faster as I hold my breath, waiting to see her.

What the fuck am I going to say?

I mean, I've thought about it. A lot. But now that I'm here, nothing I've rehearsed seems good enough.

What if she doesn't want to see me?

What if—

That thought catches in my throat as I see her step out of the driver's side.

Her long brown hair is down around her shoulders and looks like it's still damp. The pale blue scrubs she's wearing hug her body. Somehow Quinn makes anything look good. I've always thought that. But seeing her this morning, I don't think she's ever looked *this* good—a fucking sight for sore eyes, *my* sore eyes.

I watch her as she digs into the back seat and comes out with a large bag. Something falls onto the pavement and as she bends over to get it the bag on her shoulder starts to slide. I immediately open the door of my car, ready to run across and help her.

But before I can even step out and cross the street, a man comes to her rescue.

He's tall with dark hair and is wearing scrubs with a white coat.

Dr. Cartwright.

Daniel Cartwright.

I watch as he picks up the contents that fell and puts them into the bag for her, taking the other one from her shoulder and carrying it for her. She laughs as something else falls out of the back of the SUV and picks it up, throwing it back inside.

They seem happy.

He puts an arm around her shoulders and they walk into the hospital like that.

Together.

I try to make my mouth work, to call out after her, but nothing.

I try to make my feet work, to run after her, but they won't budge.

I can't.

I can't mess with her happiness.

So instead, I get back into my car and leave.

Twenty

STANDING IN MY BEDROOM, LOOKING AT MYSELF IN THE MIRROR, I ask myself the recurring question: *what the fuck am I doing?*

This time, I must've asked it out loud because I get a groan from Fergie as she watches me from the bed. She still hasn't forgiven me for abandoning her a few weeks ago. She practically lived with Lucy and Will and gained a good five pounds.

No telling what those fuckers fed her.

I finally pulled my head out of my ass a week or so ago and realized I couldn't keep sleeping at the office and avoiding everyone, including my dog. She didn't deserve that. I've apologized by taking her to the park as much as possible, but we don't go on Sundays.

That's a hard no.

"How do I look, girl?" I ask. The lazy dog rolls over onto her side, giving me the same look she gives me when I ask her what I should eat for dinner. If I had to guess, it's the dog equivalent for *I don't give a fuck*.

"Yeah, neither do I," I tell her, bending down to rub her ears.

I stand back up and look at myself again. It's not that I'm nervous, and I'm definitely not excited. I guess I'm just indifferent. I want to go and get this over with and get Sebastian off my back.

He and Lexie fixed me up with one of Lexie's co-workers, Samantha. According to Lexie, she's *pretty and funny*. Truthfully, she could be Miss Fucking America, and it wouldn't make a difference. But as long as she doesn't have an annoying laugh or look like Zach Galifianakis, I think I can handle it.

And who knows? Maybe this is exactly what I need to get out of my funk.

Or it could be a complete fucking disaster.

I'm not sure if there are any rules out there on how long you should wait to date after you get your heart trampled. It's been almost two months since I last talked to Quinn and a few weeks since that morning at the hospital when I saw her walking in with the doctor, looking happy and like everything was right in her world. So I guess it's time to move on, or at least try.

That's what I'm doing.

I'm trying.

With Samantha.

I swear, if she's annoying, I'm going to beat the shit out of Sebastian.

Actually, maybe *that's* what I need to get out of my funk.

Waiting outside the restaurant Samantha picked out, I watch people come and go.

A group of girls pass by, giggling.

A couple walks in, arm in arm.

There's a family of four walking down the sidewalk; the little girl is annoying the shit out of her brother. The mom chastises, and the dad threatens to take them both back to the car. I can't help but smile. It reminds me of my family.

Lucy is two years older than me. We've always been at the perfect age to get on each other's nerves. But I love her, and I know she loves me. She and Will have been really great these past couple of months. Outside of incessantly checking up on me, which I'm sure our mother put them up to, they've been really supportive and haven't pushed too much.

"You have got to be Jude," a voice says from behind me.

I take a deep breath and hold the smile on my face, trying to put up a good front. I remind myself that it's not this girl's fault that I don't want to be here. Who knows? Maybe she was forced into this stupid date too.

Turning around, I see a petite woman, not much taller than my sister. Her curly light brown hair frames her face and hangs down past her shoulders. Her eyes are blue, and her skin is slightly tanned, like she's recently been to the beach. When she smiles, a dimple peeks out from her cheek. She's not horrible.

"I am. You must be Samantha," I say, offering her my hand.

"I am." The sing-song reply surprisingly doesn't get on my nerves. I see the hesitancy in her eyes and recognize the reluctant way she looks at the restaurant. "So, wanna get something to eat?" she asks, pointing over her shoulder.

"Sounds great."

I really am hungry, and as we're seated at our table and the aroma of food hits me, I realize I haven't eaten since breakfast. "I'm probably getting ready to embarrass myself," I admit.

"Why?" she asks, giving me a small smile as she looks around cautiously.

Leveling her with a stare, I admit, "I haven't eaten since breakfast, so I might order half the menu."

She laughs a little, shaking her head. "Don't let me stop you," she says, motioning to the menu. "I grew up with four brothers. I'm not a stranger to a dinner table throwdown."

I laugh too, feeling the mood lighten. "Good to know."

Continuing my perusal of the menu, I take a second to check myself, wondering if there could be anything here between the two of us. Maybe I can't see it or feel it because I've been so closed off since Quinn. But even with the thorough self-examination, I don't feel anything romantic toward Samantha. However, I can admit it feels kind of nice to be out, and regardless of what happens, at least I'm going to get a good meal. I've heard nothing but good things about this place since it opened.

"I've heard the Pub Burger is amazing," Samantha says, looking down at her menu.

Glancing up at her and then back to my menu, I add, "I was just thinking I've heard really good things about the food here."

"Yeah, everyone from work has eaten here, except me." She laughs, shrugging her shoulders. "I don't get out much."

"Well, now you won't be left out."

"Yeah," Samantha says, picking up her water glass. "Cheers to that."

"Cheers to not being the lame friends."

We both laugh, taking drinks of our water.

After a few minutes, the waiter returns and takes our order. I get an appetizer and the Pub Burger, and Samantha orders a grilled chicken salad.

"You ordered a grilled chicken salad at a place known for their burgers?" I ask teasingly, or hoping it sounds that way.

"I don't like red meat," she says, scrunching her nose.

"So, you work for McDavid, have four brothers, and don't eat red meat. What else is there to know about you?" I ask. Because I'm trying. And she's nice. And I don't want to be the dick who was rude on a blind date.

"I live around the fashion district in a walk-up. Lexie and I have known each other since high school, but we hated each other back then." She laughs, pausing. "I like to do yoga, and I have a cat named Sally," she says, shrugging. "What about you?"

I chuckle, thinking about how completely different we are.

"Well, I work with Sebastian. We've known each other since college. I love extreme sports." I pause as the waiter sets down our appetizer.

"Extreme sports?" she asks.

"Yeah, like jumping out of planes, mountain biking, parasailing, bungee jumping...You name it, Sebastian and I have tried it."

Her face pales. "Are you serious?" she asks with a look of terror.

"Yeah. I love it, actually." I let out a deep breath, thinking of how alive I feel when I'm careening down a hill or watching the ground come into view from thousands of feet in the air.

That's what I need.

Just thinking about it makes me feel less...I don't know...less sad or whatever the fuck I've been feeling. I need to go jump out of an airplane or something.

"I'm terrified of heights," she says, shaking her head. "There's no way I could do anything like that."

I laugh, shrugging my shoulders. "Sebastian and I used to meet every weekend for something. Usually, rock climbing and mountain biking were our go-to's, but we're always up for something a little more *exhilarating*." I raise my eyebrows, thinking back to the sex club. *Fuck.* I haven't thought about that in a while. Looking across the table at the innocent-looking girl staring back at me, I wonder what she'd think about something like that.

Samantha is definitely no Quinn.

Nobody is Quinn, except...

The brown hair twisted in a bun is what catches my attention first, walking in the door directly behind Samantha's head of curls. It's walking past us and to a table on the other side of the restaurant.

I'd know that bun anywhere. I've pulled it down forcefully and gently untangled it...I've used it as leverage. *Fuck.* I practically groan out loud but manage to hold that shit in, barley.

What the fuck is she doing here?

"Jude?" Samantha asks.

"Yeah? What? Sorry. Thought I saw someone," I say, bringing my attention back to her and away from Quinn sitting down at a table across the room. Why did she have to come to this restaurant? Hundreds of damn restaurants in this city and she picks this one.

"I was asking about your family. Any brothers or sisters?"

"Uh, yeah, I have one sister," I say absentmindedly, unable to keep my eyes from drifting over to Quinn as she sits at the table. Then I see him. The doctor. My stomach drops, and I want to hide or run, somehow make myself disappear. I don't know where to, but I'm not sure if I can sit here. *With Samantha.* While she's sitting there. *With him.*

"What's her name?" Samantha asks, pulling my focus back to the table once again. I look across at her, and she's eyeing me like she knows my head is somewhere else. "Your sister. What's her name?"

I take a drink of my water and then pop a fried pickle into my mouth. "Lucy."

"Are you guys close?"

"Yeah," I say, nodding my head. "We're really close."

"And your parents? Do they live around here?"

Her questions calm me a bit, helping distract me. I try to keep my eyes focused on Samantha and the food. The waiter comes and brings my burger, and my stomach growls, convincing me that I can do this. Maybe Quinn won't notice me.

Maybe she will.

Do I want her to?

I chance a glance across the room as I take a large bite of my burger. She's looking at her menu. He's preoccupied with his phone. *The motherfucker.* He should be looking at her. If I were sitting there, I'd be looking at her.

"How's the burger?" Samantha asks.

Swallowing the bite, I nod my approval. "How's the salad?"

She smiles and nods. "Good. Best salad I've had in a while, actually."

"And you probably eat a lot of salads."

"Yeah." She laughs lightly as she takes a dainty bite.

We both settle into a somewhat comfortable silence as we finish our meals, each of us people-watching. Well, Samantha is people-watching. I'm Quinn-watching, but I'm trying like hell to be smooth about it.

"I'm going to the ladies' room," Samantha announces, standing from her seat. "I'll be right back."

Smiling, I stand, trying to at least appear to be a gentleman.

As soon as she's gone, I'm a little more obvious in my watching, training my eyes intently at the doctor's face as I try to gauge the mood between them. I haven't seen Quinn laugh once, although I guess she could've cracked a smile while I was trying not to watch. But something about her body language tells me she's not in a great mood. They do seem to be exchanging conversation, and I can't help wondering what it's about.

He leans back.

She leans back.

He leans forward.

She leans forward on her elbows, crossing her ankles under the table.

There's no hand-holding.

No touching.

The doctor slides out of his chair and walks toward the direction Samantha just went. To the bathroom, I presume.

Quinn must feel someone watching her because she turns her head slightly and scans the restaurant. I should look away, maybe hide behind my hand or something, but I don't.

Maybe I want her to see me.

She does.

She scans past me but does a double-take, coming right back. She doesn't seem shocked or surprised, just...sad? Indifferent? No, there's definitely emotion there. I just can't tell exactly what it is. The corners of her lips turn up into a slight smile, and she nods her head to the side as if to say "hello".

We both should look away at this point. The eye contact has lingered too long, but we don't. Not until Samantha walks past and sits across from me.

"Long line," she says, slipping back into her chair.

I glance back to see Quinn now watching Samantha. The smile on her face grows a little, but there's still something else there. I want to tell her that this is a blind date and that Samantha means nothing to me, but I can't. The doctor sits back down, and Quinn forces herself to look away. And so do I.

After I pay the bill, Samantha and I walk out the doors onto the sidewalk. She doesn't act awkward, like she's waiting on something more. I'm glad about that. She digs in her purse for her keys, and when she comes up with them, she smiles.

"I had a nice time," she says, nodding her head. "I don't usually do the blind date thing, but this wasn't so bad."

I laugh, scratching the back of my head. "Yeah, blind dates aren't my thing either."

"I can tell."

Cringing, I hate that I gave off that impression and I hope I didn't make her feel like it was her. "At least the food was good," I offer as a consolation prize.

"Definitely," she says, crossing her arms over her chest and rubbing her hands over her arms. "Good food can save a bad date."

Shit. She's probably cold and I'm now feeling like a complete asshole. "I'm sorry," I tell her. "I'm sure Lexie forced you into this."

"It wasn't horrible." Her smile is genuine and friendly, nothing more.

"I'm glad," I tell her, running a hand through my hair and feeling marginally better.

Samantha is a nice girl. Not my type, but nice. She definitely doesn't deserve to be a rebound screw. Although, my dick and I aren't quite ready for that yet anyway.

"I'll give you a good report," she says with a wink.

"I'd really appreciate that." Laughing, I shake my head, hoping Lexie doesn't grill her on Monday morning.

A split second later, Samantha's phone rings, and she holds the screen up so I can see it.

Lexie

"Damn, she didn't even wait for Monday."

"You do know Lexie, right?" she asks, arching an eyebrow.

"Yes. Probably a little too well," I admit, laughing.

If nothing else, this date with Samantha kept me from staring at the same four walls and eating a microwaveable meal. And I've laughed, which I haven't done much of in a while. For all of that, I'm grateful.

Just as I'm getting ready to say goodbye, the restaurant door opens, and out walks the doctor. He pauses, holding the door open for Quinn.

She stops when she sees Samantha and me standing there.

I see the indecision on her face, her smile faltering, so I save her the best way I know how. I walk away, leading Samantha down the sidewalk toward the parking lot.

Twenty-One

"Skydiving. This Sunday. You and Me," I tell Sebastian as I walk into his office.

"I can't." He doesn't even look up, just continues typing away on his keyboard.

"Why? Are you busy?"

"Yeah, I've got this...thing."

"With Lexie?"

"No, just a thing."

"Sundays used to be *our* thing," I say, like a bitter ex-girlfriend.

He gives me a look over his computer screen and I continue, "Sorry, it's just, I already paid for the jumps. I really need a good rush. Any chance you can reschedule your...*thing?*"

Sebastian finally pushes away from his computer and roughly scrubs at his face with his hands. "Fuck."

"What?"

He looks away, out the large window by his desk. "I can't go, because I promised Lex no more extreme sports that involve harnesses."

"What?" I ask like he just told me he has three heads or descended from aliens.

"Yeah, after the bungee jumping incident last week, she freaked out and was crying and shit, making me promise I won't do anything that requires a harness."

"What about rock climbing?" I ask, unable to wrap my brain around what he's telling me. This is not the Sebastian I know. The Sebastian I know would tell a chick to go to hell if she even tried to tell him what to order on his pizza. *What the fuck is going on around here?*

"She said rock climbing was okay, as long as it's indoors."

I plop down in the chair across from him and rake my hand through my hair.

"And before you start harping on me about being pussy-whipped, just don't, okay?"

The sharp edge to his voice tells me I shouldn't fuck with him. He's obviously just as distraught by this information as I am.

"Dude," I say, because nothing else good is coming to mind right now.

"I know."

We both sit there, staring out the window.

"You loved Quinn, right?" he asks after we've been quiet for a few minutes.

"Yeah," I answer, feeling the pinch in my chest when he refers to my feelings for Quinn in the past tense.

"You probably would've done anything for her, right?"

"Yeah." I would've. I did. I still would. But I don't admit to that, because it'd probably make me sound pathetic. Which I am. Which is also why I need to go skydiving. I need a distraction, anything to take my mind off of how pathetic I am. I also need it to remind me I'm alive and still have a beating heart in my chest.

"Well, I'll do anything for Lexie, even holding up my end of the deal to not do any extreme sports with a harness...as fucking stupid as that sounds and as much as it goes against how I normally am," he admits, exhaling.

"Even though it's a stupid fucking deal?"

"Yeah." He nods. "Even though it's a stupid fucking deal," he admits. "Lexie is it for me."

I look over at Sebastian and simultaneously want to punch him in his fucking nose and slap him on his back in congratulations. The emotions running through me are all over the board. I hate him. I'm happy for him. I wish I had what he has. I hate that I wish that. I hate that Quinn and I are over. I hate that I'm slowly forgetting how she smelled and the exact shade of brown in her eyes. I hate that it's been seventy-four days since we last talked.

And I hate that I know that.

"I get it," I finally say, standing from the chair. "I guess I'll just do two jumps. More for me." I try to force a smile and act like I'm not upset. I know it doesn't work. Sebastian always sees right through my bullshit.

"Let's go mountain biking," he suggests. "Or fuck, just hang out at the bar or something."

Slapping the door frame, I try to think if that would do it for me, but I know it won't. I need a fucking rush, one I can only get from jumping out of a perfectly good airplane. "Nah. I need this."

"Alright." He sits back in his chair and eyes me closely. "Don't do anything crazy, okay?"

"Who me?" I ask, smiling, and this time it's real, because he knows me better than to put that kind of stipulation on me.

"Whatever," he says, laughing. "Have fun. Don't die."

I laugh again, knowing deep down, he wishes he was going with me.

"I'll tell you how great it was when I get back."

"Next thing you know you'll be the one telling me about all the different pussy you're having. What the fuck is happening to us?"

I stop and turn around, staring at him.

Maybe I need to get laid.

Maybe it's time.

That's the natural progression, right?

"I don't know, dude." I shake my head and leave before he has a chance to ask me about my sex life. I'm sure he will at some point, but not today. I can't think about that today.

"Thanks, Frank," I say, shaking the old man's hand. "It was fun." I finish taking the harness off and hang it on the hooks inside the hanger. Today was a great day for jumping. The lingering adrenaline still has me flying high.

"Don't be a stranger, Jude. Bring that big oaf with you next time."

I laugh, scratching my jaw that has a week's worth of stubble. "Afraid I'll be flying solo from here on out," I say, a familiar pinch in my chest, but this time, it's due to the loss of something besides Quinn. Everything and everyone seemed to be changing.

"Oh?"

"Yeah, seems as though the big oaf has gone and fell in love and the little miss isn't so keen on him jumping out of airplanes." I smile to myself, knowing Lexie would kick my ass for the *little miss* comment, but that's okay.

She's on my shit list.

"Well, well, well. You don't say?" The old man shakes his head. "I was for sure that one would be a bachelor for life. He reminded me a lot of myself in my younger years."

"I kinda thought that myself, Frank," I admit, but happy that Sebastian found somebody all the same.

"What about you?" Frank asks, giving me a sideways glance.

Shaking my head, I work up a smile for the old man. "Nah, I'll probably be the one who's a perpetual bachelor."

Frank gives me another sideways glance. "Some pretty girl will come along one of these days…"

I just smile.

She came along, alright.

And then she left.

Twenty-Two

JIMMY SITS ANOTHER SHOT GLASS FILLED WITH TEQUILA DOWN IN front of me. No lime. I don't need no fucking lime. Or chasers. Real men just need tequila.

And it'd be nice if the fucking Mavs could win a fucking game.

"Might wanna slow your roll," Sebastian says, leaning back against the bar beside me.

"Why?" I ask, taking the shot glass and tipping it up, appreciating the slight burn it still has as it goes down, even after six shots...or was that seven?

Sebastian shakes his head and focuses on the large television across from us.

"Fucking ref! That was obviously walking. Can we not get one damned thing to go our way?" Sebastian slams his beer down on the bar and crosses his arms over his chest. "Fucking Lakers."

"We need to switch teams."

Sebastian laughs. "You'd only say that when you're drunk."

"I'm not drunk."

"Okay, tell me that again tomorrow morning when we meet with Mr. Jones."

"I'll be fine."

"Hey, Jimmy," a tall brunette says as she walks up to the bar. "How about three martinis for me and my friends?" She points over at a table where two women are sitting, waving. At me. Or maybe at Jimmy. Fuck if I know.

"How are you, handsome?" she asks, leaning against the bar on the other side of me.

I look at Sebastian and then back at her. "Who me?"

She smiles, like I'm joking. "Yes, you." Her hand touches my chest and smooths down the front of my shirt. The tie I was wearing today is hanging loose and the top few buttons are undone. Normally, I go home and change before coming to the bar, but I didn't feel like it tonight. I needed a drink more than I needed to change clothes.

"My friends and I have been watching you," she admits. "Seems as though you might need a distraction, what with all those shots you've been taking. Need to relieve some...tension?"

I look down as her long red fingernails trace a pattern on my shirt.

Why the fuck is she doing that?

"Long day," I tell her, looking up to meet her blue eyes, but they're not real. No one has eyes the color of my computer screen. They look just like that. Microsoft blue, I decide.

"Care to join us?" she asks, leaning in further until her mouth is only a few inches from mine.

A three-point shot by the Mavs makes the entire bar erupt and draws my focus to the television. As I'm turning my head to look at the woman who is now halfway sitting on my lap, I see her.

Not her. The brunette.

Well, this one is also a brunette, but that one is *my* brunette.

Or was mine.

Not mine.

But I wanted her to be.

"Quinn," I say before she's close enough to hear me.

When she notices the woman at my right, she starts to turn around, but I push her off me. "Quinn," I say louder, making her turn back around.

Her eyes meet mine and then go to the woman and then back to me. "I shouldn't have come here," she says, fidgeting with the cuff of her jacket.

"What are you doing here?" I ask, unable to filter my words or put much thought into what comes out before it does.

"I just..." She pauses and looks over her shoulder at the television and the loud fuckers yelling at it. "I knew you'd be here," she says, stepping closer so I can hear her over the noise. "Can we talk?"

I nod, but I don't know if that's my mind or my heart talking. Part of me says "fuck yes, we can talk" and the other part is saying "fuck no, go away". I don't know what part is what or what part I want to listen to, but I follow her to the door. When I'm halfway out the bar, I look back to see Sebastian watching me with a smirk on his face.

What the fuck is that for?

Fucking Sebastian, always such a cocky bastard.

I'm still cussing Sebastian in my mind when the cold air hits me and I realize it's just me and Quinn on the sidewalk outside of the bar.

"What are you doing here?" I ask again, because I can't remember if I already asked her that.

She lets out a loud sigh. "Fuck," she groans. "I don't *know* what I'm doing here."

I run a hand through my hair, trying to think clearly, but it's hard. I've wanted to talk to her ever since the last time we spoke and now, here she is and I can't seem to force myself to say the words.

What did I want to say?

What should I say?

Is she in love with Daniel? Are they happy? Did she get what she wanted? How's Henry?

But instead, I say, "I don't know why you're here either."

Why? Why did I say that?

Her big brown eyes come up to meet mine and I see it—hurt, sadness, regret. It's like I'm looking at myself in the mirror and for some reason, it pisses me off.

"I just wanted to see you...to see how you're doing."

"Well," I laugh hoarsely, spreading my arms wide. "Here I am." I feel the sarcasm and anger building up and I don't know where it's coming from, but I can't stop it.

She smiles, but it doesn't meet her eyes. It's tight and forced. We stand there for a few moments, the cold air doing wonders on my alcohol-ridden brain, sobering me up a bit.

"I know I hurt you," she finally says, wrapping her arms around herself. "And I just wanted to say I'm sorry...for all of it."

She apologizes and it's sincere. I can tell by the way she looks directly in my eyes and her jaw is set tight like she's on a mission and determined to say whatever she came here to say.

"I also want you to know that I thought I was doing the right thing and I'm sorry you got hurt in the process. I never meant for that to happen. I never meant for any of it to happen."

The familiar pinch in my chest is back and I rub it, trying to get the ache to go away. "What you mean to say is that you never meant for *me* to happen."

"You're right," she admits, letting her shoulders fall a little. "I didn't, but sometimes life is unexpected and it throws things at us we never saw coming."

"You don't have anything to apologize for. You told me not to get attached...that's all on me. I'm the one who let my heart get involved, but don't worry," I tell her. "It's uninvolved now." In my semi-drunken state, that's the best I can do. And it's a lie, but she doesn't have to know that.

Her eyes fall and so does her smile. She kicks her shoe on the concrete as we stand there in silence.

Why couldn't you have come here when I was sober?

"I'm sorry. I should've realized you'd be hanging out with Sebastian. This was just the only place I knew I could find you."

"What?"

"It's not like I came here expecting you to be...not sober," she says, somewhat defensively.

"Did I say that out loud?"

Quinn groans and rubs at her forehead. "This was a mistake."

"I fell in love with you, you know?" It's rhetorical. I don't expect her to answer, but I need her to hear it. While I have her undivided attention, I might as well tell her everything. A bitter laugh escapes as I lean over and brace my hands on my knees, trying to clear my head as much as possible. When I stand back up, I look directly into her eyes. "I loved you...even though you tried to keep me from it. I loved you anyway. And Henry," I shake my head. "I didn't even think I wanted kids before I met him."

I swallow hard to keep my emotions in check but force myself to continue. "The shitty thing is, I love that kid so much, I want what's best for him and, unfortunately, that's not me. As much as I'd love to be what's best, I know he needs his father. I can't even be mad at you, Quinn, because you're being a great mom. It just fucking sucks that I can't be what you need."

When I look back at her, there are tears streaming down her face and for some sadistic reason, it makes me happy...happy because maybe I want her to hurt as badly as she hurt me.

And sad, so fucking sad.

I'd gladly take a bullet for her.

So, the last thing I want is for her to cry.

The mixed emotions are tearing at my insides and making me want to scream.

"Daniel and I—" she starts, but I quickly shut her down. I don't think I can stomach hearing about her and Daniel and their happy family.

"Don't, Quinn...just fucking don't. I can't stand here and listen to you talk about you and Daniel, okay?" My blood starts pumping at the thought. Did she come here to rub it in my face?

I'm pissed she came here tonight. I was starting to forget, not everything, but some things. And now she shows up and her sweet and spicy scent is all I can smell, and I'm reminded that her eyes are this weird combination of gold and amber and brown and that they kind of glisten under the streetlights, especially with freshly shed tears still lingering in them.

Unable to stand another goodbye, I turn and walk back into the bar, hoping like hell she doesn't follow me.

And hoping like hell that she does.

But she doesn't.

Later, as Sebastian drives me to my apartment, I lean back against the seat and watch the buildings as we pass by. He hasn't said much since I walked back into the bar, probably assuming if I wanted to talk, I would.

His loud exhale clues me into his struggle with keeping his big trap shut.

"I know it's just killing you not to ask," I tell him, rolling my head to the other side to look at him. "So, go ahead. Let's get this over with."

"If you don't want to talk about it, it's fine."

"Bullshit. It's never fine." I sink further down in my seat, wishing I hadn't had those last two shots, but fuck me if tonight didn't turn into a shit show. "It's not fine," I murmur, meaning it in more ways than one.

It's not fine.

I'm not fine.

Quinn's not fine.

Nothing is fucking fine.

Unless we're living in some alternate universe where fine now means fucked up, then yeah, everything is *fucking fine.*

"What'd she say?" he finally asks.

"I guess she came to apologize."

"Did you at least get to tell her how you feel?"

I snort and roll my eyes, causing my head to hurt. Fucking tequila. "Yeah, I told her."

"And."

"She mentioned Daniel and I lost it. I just couldn't stand there while she talked about the two of them together. It felt like someone was twisting a knife in my chest."

After a few minutes of driving in silence, Sebastian sighs. "Well, at least you told her."

"Yeah."

I lean my head against the cool glass and close my eyes, but all I see is Quinn's tear-streaked face.

"Look at you, leaving at normal people time," Sebastian chides as we walk toward the elevator.

After my confrontation with Quinn last week, I felt like he and Lexie had me on some kind of suicide watch or something. But the truth is I've felt better this week. My chest still hurts when I think about her. I still wish things were different. But I don't feel like sleeping at the office or eating week-old food out of the break room refrigerator.

I also refuse to go on any more blind dates. I didn't have trouble finding myself dates before Quinn and when I'm ready, whenever that time comes, I'll find my own fucking dates again.

"Wanna get a beer later?" Sebastian asks, pushing "B" for the basement parking garage.

"Lexie lets you do that sort of thing?" I tease, knowing it'll get a rise out of him.

"I do what I fucking want." He adjusts his tie and stands up straighter.

I try to hold back the laugh, but I can't.

When his phone buzzes in his pocket, he can't pull it out fast enough. I watch as he reads a text message and then sits his briefcase on the floor of the elevator so he can reply quickly.

"Lexie?" I ask, keeping my head forward and walking out of the elevator when the doors open.

"Yeah. I've gotta pick up kale on my way home." He sounds disgusted and maybe confused.

Sebastian does not eat green stuff.

"Kale is kinda like lettuce. You'll find it in the produce." I'm kind of teasing, but also helping a brother out, just in case he doesn't know. "But you do what you want." I hide the laugh this time, but not the grin. I can't.

"Shut the fuck up."

"After you pick up your kale, call me and we'll grab a beer."

"I hate you."

"Enjoy your kale," I call out over my shoulder as we go our separate ways.

"Fuck you," he calls back.

We could do this all day. We're like twelve-year-olds with jobs.

When I reach for the handle on my car door, my pocket buzzes and I'm pretty certain it's Sebastian. Always needing one last *fuck you*. If my feelings for Quinn weren't so raw still, he'd probably even tease me about how he's getting pussy and I'm not, because that trumps everything...even kale.

Pulling my phone out of my pocket, I start my car, trying to think of a good comeback before I open the text message.

But it's not from Sebastian.

Emergency

Twenty-Three

QUINN

"Hey, Brenda, I'm gonna go take a nap. Text me if you need me."

"No problem, Quinn."

I quickly make my way down the hall and enter the break room, hoping to find it empty. It's pretty quiet right now in the ER, and I know Brenda, the nurse practitioner, has things under control, so I should be able to get a somewhat decent nap. Of course, that can all change in a matter of seconds, but I'm so tired I have to try at least.

Sleep is a hot commodity.

As I push open the door to the sleeping area, I'm relieved to find it empty. It's more of a closet than a room, but it's dark and quiet, and the bunk beds are pretty comfy. Now, I just have to see if my mind will relax long enough to allow me a few blessed hours of reprieve.

Every time I close my eyes lately, all I see is Jude's face.

Not the gorgeous face I'd grown accustomed to seeing a few times a week—lustful eyes, a mouth that is equal parts fun-loving smile and cocky-bastard smirk, and a jaw you could cut glass with—but the face he wore when he told me I broke his heart. The look on his face as he put it all out there was heartbreaking. He was so vulnerable, something I'd only caught a glimpse of that day in the park when I told him about Daniel.

I can't get either of those images out of my brain, and I don't want to, because I know I deserve it. He said it was all on him, but he's wrong. He's not to blame; this is all on me. And I wish I could take it away somehow.

I hate that I hurt him. I never meant to. I never meant for him to have feelings for me. I never meant to have feelings for him. But life is funny that way.

Breaking things off with Jude was one of the hardest things I've ever done, but I did what I thought I had to do—for myself, but mostly for Henry. The truth of the matter is that I'd sacrifice everything to give my son what he needs, even my own happiness.

Of course, I can't deny how foolish I was. I've done a lot of foolish things in my life. My number one was assuming Daniel and I would pick up where we left off six years ago. That was very naïve. I wasn't in love with him back then, and I'm not in love with him now, but I've always held on to the hope of *maybe*.

Maybe he'll come back.

Maybe he'll be excited about being a dad.

Maybe we'll fall in love.

Maybe I'll finally have the family my father wanted me to have.

My dad loved Daniel. He was the son Quincy Roland never had. When my dad died, Daniel and I sort of fell into each other, using each other for support. I thought it was meant to be, that even from beyond the grave, my father was still somehow orchestrating it all. But then Daniel was gone too.

Should I have told Daniel about the pregnancy? Of course.

Was I scared shitless when I finally did tell him about Henry? Absolutely.

As I roll over onto my side, the memories from the past few weeks flood my mind.

They've been full of surprises.

For all of us.

Daniel has always been responsible and trustworthy. It's something my father admired about him and something I'd always appreciated as well. It's what made us friends.

So, I banked on that friendship seeing me through as I told him about *our son*.

More than anything, I wanted to right my wrongs and tell Daniel everything I should've told him six years ago. He needed to know the truth and I needed the chance to see if there was anything left between us, even a spark. I owed that to Henry. But I couldn't, in good conscience, do that while leaving Jude hanging on the side, which is why I had to end things between us. As much as I tried to not fall for him, I was...I did. Had Daniel not come back, who knows what might've happened between us—Jude and me, that is.

Because, news flash: there were zero sparks between Daniel and me.

One night after he got back to Dallas, my mom had taken Henry to the movies while Daniel and I caught up over dinner and a bottle of wine. With liquid courage running through my veins, I told him everything.

I told him how I found out I was pregnant a week after he moved away.

I told him I tried to call him many times but usually chickened out and hung up.

I admitted to not wanting him to think I was trapping him and that I also didn't want to hold him back in his career.

You have a son and he's the best thing in the world.

After explaining all of it, I apologized profusely for keeping Henry from him, and then I sat back and braced myself for the fallout.

We sat for a few minutes in silence, and with a dazed and confused kind of look on his face, he finally asked to see a picture of Henry. I watched as he scanned the photo, obviously noticing the resemblance, because it's damn hard to miss. Daniel could try to deny Henry is his, but the darker skin and dimples did not come from me.

As he continued to look at the picture, he started asking questions about him.

Of course, I was thrilled to answer them and before he left, I ended up showing him just about every picture ever taken of Henry—from birth to this past Christmas.

Daniel showed more forgiveness and acceptance than I ever could've hoped for.

He was understandably hurt and pissed I'd kept Henry from him all these years, but he said he understood...or that he was trying to, at least, which was all I could ask. He also admitted it was probably best if he wasn't introduced to Henry that night because he needed to go home and absorb everything, which made me feel nothing but relief. I didn't want to rush anything with their introduction and was hoping for a little time to talk to Henry by myself first.

When I walked him to the door, with a picture of Henry in hand, he stopped at the first step and said there was something he needed to tell me too.

Turns out, Daniel is gay.

He and his partner, Zach, have been together for five years. Zach is actually the reason Daniel took the cardiac position at Mercy. He's an IT guy and was recently offered a job at a large oil and gas company in Dallas.

Since that night, we've been hanging out a few times a week. Sometimes it's just the two of us; other times, Henry is with us. Zach has even joined us for dinner a couple of times, and it's been great seeing Daniel truly happy.

The best part is seeing his love for our son.

I smile as I think about my sweet boy.

"Mom, why is Daniel coming over again? I want Jude to come over instead. He's never even been here. He can bring Fergie, and she can play with me in my room. I'll pick my Legos up so she doesn't eat them. I promise."

It hurts to disappoint him, especially when he gives me that pouty face that normally would make me giggle, but I have to stand firm. The truth is, I'd much rather have Jude over than Daniel, but tonight's the night we tell Henry that he's Daniel's son, and I can't be distracted by my other mistakes. I have to try to fix this one first.

"Sweetie, Jude and Fergie can't come over. We have plans with Daniel. Besides, we've already promised Daniel we'd watch Return of the Jedi *with him tonight."*

My son rolls his eyes and makes a "tsk" sound. "I can't believe he hasn't watched all the Star Wars *movies, Mom. I mean, where'd you find this guy? He's not as cool as Jude."*

My heart sinks at the mention of Jude's name. Again. To be honest, it's been hard watching the Star Wars *movies since ending things with Jude simply because of that damn Stormtrooper toy he gave Henry. On more than one occasion, I've caught myself looking at it and thinking about what he must've gone through to get it for Henry, making me smile like a damn loon. The smile soon fades as realization sinks in, and I force myself to get a grip.*

Stupid fucking Stormtrooper.

Stupid fucking me.

"Is Daniel your new boyfriend?" Henry's question catches me off guard, but it's an easy one to answer.

"No, Henry. He's not. But he's very important to our family. I hope you'll give him a chance. He really is a good guy."

"Okay, Mom. I'll try. I still wish Jude was your boyfriend, though."

Without a reply, I kiss Henry on the top of his head before heading back to the kitchen. What would I say anyway? Jude was never my boyfriend to begin with, and I doubt he wants anything to do with me now. I've made a complete mess of my life yet again, but I have to put Henry's needs before mine.

Daniel and I told Henry the truth later that night, and he took it well. It was almost as if he suspected it all along. The serious moment quickly lightened as soon as Henry exclaimed, "So, that's where I get my dimples from!"

As I tucked him into bed after Daniel went home, Henry asked again if Daniel was my boyfriend.

"Now will Daniel be your boyfriend?"

"No, baby. Daniel will never be my boyfriend, but he will always *be your dad," I assure him.*

"But don't you want a boyfriend?"

My heart melts at the concerned look on his face. "Maybe one of these days, but right now, I have my hands full with you." I give his belly a tickle before kissing him good night and closing his door behind me.

Once I'm in bed, I plug my phone into its charger, sadness sinking in again as my screen lights up with only my screen saver, no "emergency" texts from Jude.

I must have dreamed of Jude while I napped because I wake up with the usual throb between my legs. No man has ever made me feel the way he did—in the bedroom or out—and I long to be with him again, to feel his body pressed against mine and watch his face as he enters me.

Squeezing my thighs together, I try to relieve the ache and think of something other than Jude. There's no way I'm going to rub one out while I'm at work. I have to get my body under control before I start seeing patients.

The sound of a woman's anguished voice filters through the wall, officially breaking me from my Jude-spell, and I quickly gather myself and run down the hall to see if I can help.

Before I get around the corner, recognition floods my brain at not only the sound of the woman's voice, but other voices as well.

Holy shit, the Harrises are here.

In my ER.

I peek into the lobby and see Lucy hugging Will before my gaze falls on Jude. He's heartbreakingly beautiful as he holds his weeping mother, while also listening to...*Daniel?*

Oh, my God. Keith.

He's the only one missing from the group, and seeing Daniel standing there, in doctor mode...It can only mean one thing.

Knowing there's nothing for me to do here, medically, I allow myself to watch Jude a little longer. Seeing him both hurts and heals my heart, and I know I need to leave before I get caught. As I start to back away, Susan leaves Jude's arms and hugs Daniel.

I'm fascinated by the way Jude's jaw clenches at that moment, but I force myself to keep retreating until I realize that Susan is now watching me. My eyes widen, and hers soften, causing me to turn around and run back into the staff lounge.

Coward.

I hole up and avoid the hallways as long as possible, worried about Keith but afraid to insert myself into Jude's family, even though I miss them. It's only an hour later when Susan finally corners me outside the cafeteria, like she'd been seeking me out.

"Quinn! I'm so happy I ran into you," she says as she pulls me into a bone-crushing hug.

Giving in to it, I bask in her embrace, hugging her back tightly. "How is Keith? I saw you speaking with D—Dr. Cartwright. Is it his heart? Is he okay?" All of my concerns come flooding out.'

"Oh, he's fine." She waves her hand like she's swatting a bug away. "The man thought he was having a heart attack. Scared us all to death, I swear! Turns out, it was just gas."

My eyes widen and I practically choke on air. "I'm sorry, what?"

"You heard me," she says, quirking an eyebrow and shaking her head. "After he was finally in a room, hooked up to every machine possible, he ripped the loudest fart known to man. I'm surprised the hospital is still standing." Annoyance and amusement are shown equally in her face, but I also recognize the pure love and relief she feels. I can't help but wonder how Jude is feeling and whether or not he's still here.

As if she can read my mind, Susan tells me, "Jude is still with him in the

ER, you know. I'm sure he'd love to see you."

"I'm pretty sure he wouldn't." I shake my head adamantly. "I don't know if he's told you anything about us, but we stopped seeing each other a few months ago." Most people probably think seeing each other means dating, but I'm confident Susan Harris knows exactly what that means pertaining to me and her son. It's more tactful and respectful than saying I'm no longer fucking your son. Although it felt like so much more, but that's something I've tried to avoid thinking about and now is definitely not the time.

"He told me, but that doesn't mean anything. I see his face when he hears your name and I saw *you* when you were watching him in the lobby. You both need to get your heads out of your asses and talk to each other."

Don't hold back, Susan.

My heart clenches at the memory of our interaction at the bar a week ago. "I've tried to talk to him...He wouldn't listen."

"Well, you're just gonna have to make him listen." The way she looks at me, like she's conspiring with secret forces, causes me to take a step back. "I have the perfect plan," she says, clapping her hands before grabbing my arm and pulling me to a nearby bench.

"I don't know," I say, shaking my head as she forces me down beside her. I've only been around Susan a couple of times, but it was long enough to know she's a force to be reckoned with. Her having a plan makes my stomach twist into a knot.

"You remember how an auction works, right?"

Twenty-Four

JUDE

ARE YOU ALMOST HERE?

After quickly glancing at the text from my sister, I roll my eyes and toss my phone back in the passenger seat. Lucy obviously has something up her sleeve because she's been pestering me all week about whether or not I'll be at this week's Sunday dinner.

Like I'd miss it.

After Dad's scare last week, I'm back to making Harris Family Dinners a priority.

My stomach drops just thinking back on that day. When I first got the text, my Quinn-fueled tunnel vision made me only see the word "emergency". It took me a minute to see the rest of the message, where my sister told me they were taking my dad to Mercy.

In that initial split second, when I thought the message was from Quinn, I felt very conflicted. Part of me was elated to hear from her and was ready to meet her at the hotel, but then my common sense kicked in. I was pissed and hurt that she would think I'd immediately jump into our old arrangement without another thought.

Once my vision cleared and I read the rest of the text, all thoughts of Quinn fell to the wayside, and I headed to the hospital. I hadn't even thought about being at Quinn's place of employment until I saw Dr. Cartwright step into the waiting room to talk to my mom. I was less than thrilled to see him but knowing he's one of the best cardiologists in the state made me relieved he was helping my dad.

My dad, who should be able to tell the difference between a heart attack and gas at his age.

Thinking about the expression on my mom's face when he ripped *the big one*, as it is now referred to and will forever be known as, in his room has me chuckling to myself.

I swear, my family is crazy, but I love them.

Once I knew my dad would be okay, I took a little stroll around the ER to see if Quinn was working. Cindy busted me and let me know she was on her dinner break. I never did see her there, but I guess it was for the best.

I said my piece in my drunken state the other night, and I don't regret it.

Mentally, I kicked myself when I sobered up, wishing I'd just heard her out. I know how it feels to have things you need to say to somebody and I hate that I didn't just man up and listen to her. When it's all said and done, I hope one of these days I can see Quinn out somewhere and be cordial. Regardless of everything that's happened, I still want only the best for her.

Even if that's Daniel.

But I feel like the ball is in her court now. I can't keep chasing after her or pining away for her anymore. I have to get my shit together, and if she wants to talk more, she knows where to find me.

When I get to my parent's house, my mother greets me at the door, and I make sure to squeeze a little bit harder when she hugs me. For as aggravated as she was with my father's ER fiasco, I know she was worried about him and scared about the what-ifs. She has since put him on a strict diet, just to be safe, but I can't help but wonder if it's really her form of punishment for him putting her through so much grief.

"Come in, Jude. Your sister is up to something, and I need you to distract her before I lose my damn mind."

"Sure thing, Mom," I say before kissing the top of her head. "How's Dad?"

"Oh, he's fine. He's in the living room watching the game. I'm surprised you didn't hear him cussing at the television from the driveway."

As soon as I'm inside, my mom hurries off to the kitchen, and I head into the living room, where the television is loud, and the voices of my family

NO STRINGS ATTACHED 163

members are even louder. Both my dad and Will are yelling at the referees on the screen, and Lucy is practically shouting into her cell phone at some poor soul. When she looks up and sees me, she quickly hangs up and greets me with a hug.

"I'm so happy you're here, Jude! Mom kicked me out of the kitchen, and these two are driving me insane with their basketball nonsense."

"Baby, it's not nonsense," Will corrects. "It's the Mavs."

"Hey, son. Good to see you." My father stands, hugging me tightly, and I'm relieved that he still feels strong in my arms. There was a moment when he looked weak and frail when he was in the ER, and it really shook me up. "I want to talk to you about something, Jude. I need your help."

"Sure, Dad. Whatever you need."

He claps his hands together, and with an excited gleam in his eyes, he says, "I need you to hook me up with your bungee-jumping guy."

"Oh, hell no," my mother says, cutting him short. She's standing in the doorway with her hands on her hips. I can practically see the steam shooting out of her ears. "Keith David Harris, I forbid you to bungee jump or do any other foolish activity!"

My dad huffs. "Woman, you're already making me eat rabbit food. You can't tell me what I can and can't do with my free time."

"Like hell I can't! Just because you passed the biggest fart this side of the Mississippi does not mean you've been given a new lease on life." My mom glares at my dad, and I have a feeling this has been a common argument between them lately.

"You don't get this worked up when Jude does his crazy shit," he accuses.

She sighs, crossing her arms over her chest. "I'm always worried about Jude when he goes on his adventures, but not once has he scared me the way you did the other night. I thought I was going to lose you, and I can't go through that again!" Seeing my mom burst into tears catches everyone off guard. It's just not something we've seen her do often, and it makes us all realize how upset she really is.

My dad immediately embraces her, trying to soothe her with soft words and gentle caresses. He leads her down the hall, leaving Lucy, Will, and me standing in the living room, bewildered.

"What the hell just happened?" Will asks, finally breaking the silence.

"I don't know, man. I don't think I've ever seen that kind of outburst from my parents," I admit. They've always been affectionate with each other in front of us, but any less-than-perfect issues they've had in their relationship have always been handled behind the scenes.

"Well, I'm going to go check on them," Lucy declares, quickly walking out of the room.

"Leave them be! They'll be fine," Will yells to his wife's retreating form. Seeing that his words had no effect on her, he turns to me and asks, "Ready for a beer?"

"Hell yes," I answer, slapping him on the shoulder and following him into the kitchen.

Just as I pop the top off my bottle, my sister rushes in with an annoyed expression on her face.

"What's wrong? Are Mom and Dad okay?" I ask.

"Oh, yeah. They're *just* fine," she says in an exasperated tone, with a little huff at the end for good measure. "They're currently screwing each other's brains out in the bathroom!"

I don't know why Lucy is so surprised. It's not the first time our parents have excused themselves from a room for a quickie. "Well, at least they're not yelling at each other."

Lucy snorts. "Remember that time you had friends staying the night and one of them thought Mom and Dad were fighting in the middle of the night."

"Yeah, he called his dad," I add, the memory making me laugh. "Who was a cop."

Lucy is now laying over the kitchen counter laughing. "Oh, God. I remember them showing up and banging on the door. Mom and Dad both came hurrying down the stairs half-dressed. The look on that cop's face was priceless."

"Y'all know this could be a while," Will says, grabbing another beer. "I'm starving."

"Yeah, let's go ahead and fix our plates. I'm sure they won't mind," Lucy says, reaching up to kiss his cheek.

The three of us are seated at the table and about to start eating when our parents saunter into the kitchen. My mom's hair looks like a rat's nest, and my dad's chest is puffed out like a fucking peacock. Neither one of them has the common decency to pretend to look ashamed either.

"Oh, I'm so glad you all went ahead and fixed your plates," Mom tells us. "Keith, honey, are you ready for some chicken fried steak and mashed potatoes?"

So much for rabbit food.

Once everyone is settled and tucked into their food, the atmosphere is lighter. It feels the way our Sunday dinners felt before the infamous trip to the ER, and it's a huge relief.

"Jude, dear, don't forget to have your tux cleaned before the bachelor auction next week. I just know you're going to bring in some big bucks for the charity Will and I are working with."

Shit. I'd forgotten about the auction and that I'd promised Mom I'd volunteer. The idea of being back up on the block makes me nervous as fuck, I'm not gonna lie, but I can't let Mom and Will down. Especially since she just broke down in the living room. Besides, how much harm can a little charity auction be? I'm sure it'll just be a bunch of old women with big pocketbooks.

"No problem, Mom. I'll be there."

She smiles while reaching across to pat my hand. I smile back reassuringly, still trying to choke down the uneasy feeling I get when I think about it.

Lucy clears her throat and wipes her mouth with her napkin. I'd say she's nervous by the way she's fidgeting, but I can't imagine what for. "Before we have dessert," she says, pushing her chair back a little, "Will and I have an announcement to make."

The two of them look at each other and smile before turning back to us and exclaiming, "We're pregnant!"

Pandemonium erupts as my parents start jumping and squealing and crying along with my sister and her husband. I'm extremely happy for Lucy and Will. Thrilled, in fact, but I can't help but be reminded of how I could've had a family of my own if everything had worked out the way I'd wanted.

The pain in my chest feels like I'm having a heart attack...or maybe it's gas...or maybe it's the fact that I still miss Quinn and Henry so fucking much it hurts.

Once all the hugs have been given and my mom breaks out champagne for everyone except Lucy, I decide now is as good a time as any to share my good news.

"Since we're celebrating," I say after taking a large gulp of the champagne, wishing it was whiskey, "I have a little announcement of my own."

My mom tilts her head with a warm smile on her face. "What is it, honey?"

"I'm buying a house."

"That's great, Jude," my dad says, reaching over and gripping my shoulder.

"Yep, put an offer on it a few days ago and just got a call that they accepted it." A while back, I felt completely satisfied with my life, but Quinn helped me realize I want more. I want a house that will eventually feel like a home, and I want a family.

This is step one.

"Somewhere close?" my sister asks.

"Actually, it's not far from here. Just a couple miles down the road."

"Well, that's wonderful, honey," my mom says, tears springing up in her eyes again, and I'm glad they're happy ones this time. The moisture in her eyes actually travels down her cheek, and I think about getting up and going to her, but my dad's there, pulling her into his chest.

"Sorry," she says, her voice cracking. "It's just one of the best feelings to have you all here today and with such exciting, wonderful news. I'm just...I'm so happy."

My dad kisses her temple and rubs her shoulder.

I glance over at Lucy and Will, who are pretty much mimicking them.

I want that.

I want what they have.

And I'll get it one of these days.

I've had a taste, and now I know I want it all.

Twenty-Five

JUDE

Staring at myself in the long mirror of the dressing room my mom put me in, I straighten my bow tie. The nerves I've had for the last week are present and accounted for, but I can't turn back now. Besides, my mom would kill me if I decided to bolt. Plus, it's for charity, so I'll suck it up, walk out there, smile, turn, and hopefully bring in a little cash for a good cause.

Sebastian and Lexie are here tonight. They promised to bid on me if I'm met with crickets. I decided the only thing worse than being bought by a white-haired cougar would be to not be bid on at all.

A guy sticks his head in to tell me and another dude that we've got five minutes.

I really wish they wouldn't do that. Something about it makes my palms sweat a little more and my heart beat a little faster. It's like when you're getting ready to jump out of a plane. It's better to not think about it...no countdown... just walk out onto the bar, and you jump.

"Right this way, Mr. Harris," the guy says, leading me to the opening in the curtain.

"Hey, baby." My mom sneaks up beside me, wrapping an arm around my shoulder.

"Hey, Mom." I hug her and take comfort in her being here. "I thought you'd be off...coordinating or whatever."

She laughs and nudges me as we watch one of the other lucky bachelors strut around on the stage. "I just had to come back here and wish you good luck."

"No worries," I tell her with a wink. "I've done this before."

She shakes her head and laughs. "You've always been my risk-taker," she whispers, both of us still watching the stage. "I love that about you."

"I'm sure it's given you more gray hairs than you'd like to admit," I tell her, laughing quietly.

"Eh, maybe, but it's worth it." She wraps an arm around my waist and pulls me closer. "There's something I want you to promise me," she whispers.

"What's that?" I ask. She should know by now that I'd do just about anything for her.

"Promise me you'll still jump...when the time comes...still jump."

When I look down, she's staring back at me with more sincerity than I know what to do with. We both know she's not talking about an airplane or a bridge. I'm not sure what brought on this heart-to-heart, but it's hitting me right in the gut for some reason. Trying to keep my emotions in check, I simply nod and kiss the top of her head.

"Next up," the emcee says, "we have Jude Harris. He's a graduate of Texas A&M University..." The rest of his words fall on deaf ears as I step out onto the stage. On the outside, I'm all smiles and head nods. Occasionally, I hear the crowd cheer, and I assume it's the peanut gallery, also known as Sebastian, Lexie, Will, and Lucy.

"Take it off," someone shouts from my left. Sebastian. There're a few laughs from the audience, and several catcalls follow.

The emcee asks me to walk to the edge of the stage and turn to give the audience a good look at what they're bidding on.

I really can't believe I agreed to this. There's a hum—an energy—that feels all too familiar and takes over the room. I lick my lips and let out a deep breath, trying to ready myself.

"Can I get one hundred dollars?" the emcee asks.

"One hundred," a woman's voice in the front row calls out. The lights are bright, but due to her proximity, I can see her perfectly curled blonde hair. She's probably my mother's age, and I can't help but laugh. This is crazy. Not the craziest thing I've done, but still.

"Two hundred," calls another mature-sounding voice from the middle of the crowd.

"Two fifty," calls another from my right.

The fact that there are people bidding and they're not my best friend or my sister has me shaking my head.

"Five hundred dollars," calls a voice from the back.

I strain my eyes, shielding them from the lights to see better.

Swallowing hard, I try to keep it together. I'd know that voice anywhere.

"Five fifty," the blonde in the front says.

"Six," the familiar voice in the back calls.

"Seven," the blonde retorts as she turns in her seat to see her competition, the tone of her voice taking on an offensive edge.

"One thousand dollars," the voice in the back counters.

Gasps and whispers fill the room as everyone tries to see who's doing the bidding.

"Do I hear one thousand fifty?" the emcee asks, pleasantly surprised at the money on the table. "One thousand fifty?" the emcee asks once more to the lady in the front row, giving her one last chance to bid, but I don't hear her response.

My attention is focused on the back of the room as I watch a man go to the woman in red and take her out the side door. I look around and try to find a fast way off the stage. The guy who had been corralling us backstage walks up and directs me back to where I came from. I try to walk the other way, but he tightens his hold on my arm.

"I need to go to that woman...the one who bid on me," I tell him, feeling somewhat out of breath. I'm not sure why, but I think I've been holding it since the five-hundred-dollar bid was called out. "I need to see her."

"You will, Mr. Harris," he assures me.

"No, now," I insist, pulling my arm free. "Where did they take her?" I look around for the exit.

"Down the hall to the right," he says, pointing over his shoulder with a puzzled look on his face. "Is everything all right?"

"Yeah," I tell him, practically shoving him out of my way. "It's fine."

It's fine.

There's that phrase again.

But somehow, with her in the room, it feels like it could be fine.

I don't know why she's here.

I don't know why she bid on me.

But she's here.

For me.

And I need to talk to her. I need to see her.

I run down the hall and turn the corner, colliding with brown hair and golden-brown eyes and a red dress that might kill me.

Bracing her and myself, I try to keep us both upright. My arms are wrapped around her shoulders and she laughs into my chest. "Sorry," I say, backing up and giving her some space.

"I'm sorry," she says, and it feels like it means more than this...her running into me, or maybe I ran into her.

Maybe we collided into each other, like a fucking free fall.

We stand there for a second, taking each other in, a hum in the air, like electricity flowing through currents. "Thank you," I finally tell her, breaking the silence.

"For what?" she asks, her brows pulling together.

"For saving me from Blondie."

"Oh," she says, dropping her tone and her lids. "She had plans for you." Her laugh takes me aback and sets me at ease all at the same time. I watch as she leans her shoulder against the wall. Her face slowly fades from a laugh to serious business. "Listen." She pauses and looks down toward her feet. I follow her gaze and notice her sparkly red shoes. No combat boots. "I came here tonight because I need to talk to you."

"You could've just called," I tell her. "It's a lot cheaper than bidding a thousand bucks on me."

I say it like I'm teasing, but I'm serious.

She could've had me for free from the beginning.

"I know." She nods her head and swallows hard. "I just needed you to listen, and now you don't have a choice, because technically, you're mine for the rest of the evening."

Trying not to let my hopes get too high, I nod. "I see."

"It's as if we've done this before." She smiles, and I smile. And we both chuckle.

"So, now that you have me, what are you going to do with me?" I ask, cocking my head.

She purses her lips and I see a million emotions pass across her beautiful face. "Can we talk?"

"Sure." I cross my arms over my chest and lean against the wall next to her. Here seems as good a place as any. My self-preservation is kicking in, and as much I'm happy to see her and as much as I want her, I want to hear what she has to say first before I'll agree to anything else.

I'm not chasing.

But I'm not running either.

"Okay," Quinn says, looking around, but the hallway is empty. It's just the two of us. She lets out a deep breath, and I hate the pain that's now in her eyes. "I don't know where to start." Her voice is suddenly small and thick with emotion. "But just know that I'm sorry. I know I said this the other night, but I want you to hear it while you're sober." She pauses, taking another deep breath and then releasing it.

"For what?" I ask, trying not to sound defensive but failing, because her just saying sorry isn't good enough. I need answers.

"For everything. For being naïve. For shutting you out. For lying to myself." There are tears in her eyes, and she bites down on her lip to keep from crying. "I'm also really sorry I took Henry away from you." She sniffles and wipes away a tear with the back of her hand. "He really misses you...and Fergie."

We stand there in silence for a few minutes.

"I have to know why, Quinn. Why couldn't you just let me love you?"

She shakes her head, tears beginning to slip out of her big brown eyes and down her cheeks faster than she can keep up, but she doesn't turn away or hide. "I was scared." She shrugs as her lip quivers. "I've been scared for so long. After my dad died and my relationship with Daniel turned out like it did, I felt like I was better off not letting anyone else in. I don't know why...I thought if I kept everyone at a distance and put armor around my heart, it wouldn't get broken again. The beat-up bug...the combat boots...the club... they were all ways of not attaching myself to people. It worked for a while, but then you walked in, and it happened anyway. I got attached...and then I threw it all away." The sob she lets out nearly severs me in two. "And I'm so fucking sorry."

I stand there, watching her beautiful face crumble in sadness, along with her walls, and it breaks my heart all over again, because regardless of the shit that's happened, I still love her.

I love her beat-up bug and her combat boots.

I love the girl who thinks she's scared but is actually really brave.

I love the girl who cares about other people's lives more than her own.

I especially love the love she has for Henry.

I love her fierceness and protectiveness.

I love the way she comes undone beneath me.

I love that she'd rather have a hamburger than a salad and that she shoots tequila straight.

She's not perfect.

But I don't want perfect.

I want her.

Flaws and all.

Unable to stand it any longer, I pull her to me, and she slowly begins to melt into my chest. Her shoulders relax and I feel her entire body shudder. But what I feel the most is an immediate sense of wholeness. Having her this close is a soothing balm.

I love the way she fits so perfectly in my arms.

As I rest my head on top of hers and hold her tight, my mom's words from earlier come back to me.

Promise me you'll still jump.

When you fall in extreme sports...when your equipment fails you or you crash and burn, the best thing you can do is get back out there and do it again. Because if you don't, fear and what-ifs will keep you from taking risks. And without risks, we never truly live.

"Maybe I should've fought harder," I whisper against her hair. "You fight for what you love. I shouldn't have let my fear of losing you keep me from telling you how I felt."

We stand there for so long my legs begin to burn from holding us both up and staying in the same position. Quinn's sobs stopped a while ago, but her hold on me hasn't loosened. I lean back and try to get a look at her face to judge her emotional stability, but she squeezes tighter.

"Don't look at me," she mumbles into my chest, her voice raspy from crying. "I'm hideous."

I laugh and then feel the shake of her shoulders against me. "You're never hideous." It's the truth. Even when I wanted to hate her, I couldn't. I fell in love with the girl who didn't want me to, not to spite her, but in spite of her... in spite of the walls, in spite of the heartache, in spite of the circumstances...I fell in love with her anyway. "I love you," I whisper.

"Still?"

"Always." I sigh, pulling her even tighter. "Even if you don't want me to. Even if you marry Daniel."

Fifty years from now, regardless of what happens, there will still be a piece of my heart that she owns.

"I'm not marrying Daniel."

My body stills; my heart beats a little faster.

"I was never meant to marry Daniel. That was just another wall I put up. I think I always knew it, but it took me a while to see it." She lets out a deep sigh and melts deeper into my chest. "Even if Daniel had proposed, I would've said no," she says firmly, pulling her head back and looking straight in my eyes. "I need you to know you're not my second choice or some consolation prize. You're the only choice."

My lips crash into hers, a little more forcefully than necessary, because I need to feel her. I need to know this is real—that she's here and that her words aren't some figment of my imagination.

"You love me?" I ask against her lips.

"I do," she says, kissing my jaw.

"Tell me." I *need* to hear her say it.

"I love you, Jude. I've loved you for longer than I know, because you snuck up on me and jumped over my walls before I even knew what hit me." She kisses me again, and then our lips still as we breathe each other in.

"I love you."

Epilogue

7 MONTHS LATER

"Jude! Henry!"

The cute kid sitting beside me, who's nestled down into the couch, just looks up and snickers. "Maybe she'll think we disappeared," he whispers.

"Doubt it, dude. She probably saw the car in the driveway."

Fergie's feet click-clack on the floor and quickly round the corner, greeting Quinn at the door.

"Hey, girl," Quinn says. The two of them have formed a female alliance. Somehow Fergie gets votes and shit. Not sure how that happened. "Where are the boys?"

The big-ass dog runs back down the hallway and straight into the family room, selling us out.

"She can't not keep a secret," Henry says, giggling beside me.

Pretty sure those not's cancel each other out, but I let it slide. I've learned over the months there's no sense arguing with him. His little-kid rationalization always wins.

"Were you two hiding from me?" Quinn asks, coming to stand between us and the television.

"No," Henry says in his higher-pitched voice, the one he uses when he's lying. He's a horrible liar, just like his mother.

I smile up at Quinn, letting my eyes rake over her. The light-blue scrubs are my favorite, and she knows it.

"Why don't you go pick up the Legos in your room? We've got dinner at MeMe and Pop's house tonight," I tell Henry, ruffling his hair.

"MeMe and Pop's! Yay!" he exclaims, hands in the air. "Will Penelope be there?"

"Nah, they'll just leave her at home," Quinn teases.

Henry's excited behavior halts as he looks up at Quinn with wide eyes. "Seriously?"

Seriously. It's his new favorite word.

"Sure, I bet she'll just sleep anyway," I say, joining in the ruse with Quinn. We're horrible parents.

Parents. It took me a while to go from Jude, the cool guy, to Jude, the step-dad, but I'm *so* there. Something that seemed so far away and completely off my radar was exactly what I needed in my life. I just didn't know it. At least not until Quinn and Henry showed up. She says I snuck into her life. Well, she snuck into mine too, right through the back door. I wasn't looking for love or a family or any of that, but I found it...or it found me.

Regardless, I'm never letting them go.

"Jude," Henry warns, turning to me. "Aunt Luce would not leave Penelope at home alone," he says, shaking his head. "MeMe wouldn't let her."

"You don't think so?"

"No way, dude. Seriously."

"Yeah, true. Well, I guess she'll be there, then."

"Sweet!"

Sweet is another new word he uses constantly. He picked that one up from Sebastian. Between Daniel, Zach, Sebastian, Will, and my dad, Henry has a lot of bad influences. It's surprising he's such a good kid.

After he takes off down the hall to his bedroom, Quinn looks at me with a smile. "Maybe we should leave him at home?" she teases, plopping down beside me and taking Henry's place under my arm.

"Maybe we should leave him with MeMe and Pops," I counter. "You're off tomorrow, right?" Pulling her to me, I kiss the top of her head and then her temple...and then just below her ear, where it makes her squirm.

"On call," she says, distracted by my lips.

Moving farther down, kissing her neck, I growl. "I'll take it." In one swift move, I have her under me, lifting her hips, wanting more than I'm able to give her right now. My cock grinds into her heat anyway, begging for release.

It's been less than twelve hours, but he's needy. For her. Always.

"Mom!" Henry calls from his room, making us freeze. "I can't find my lightsaber. The blue one!"

"In your closet!" Quinn yells back.

We stay still for a moment, listening to a door opening and rummaging and then, "Found it!"

Quinn laughs, looking up at me. "We've only got thirty minutes, and I need a shower."

"I'd like to say I'd join you, but we already know that takes longer than thirty minutes."

She groans. "And Henry would be asking what we're doing in the bathroom together."

Yeah, we've had to get creative with our alone time and our lies we tell when we get caught.

"Rain check?" she asks.

"I'll be cashing in tonight," I assure her, kissing her so hard she groans in pleasure.

"MeMe!" Henry calls as we walk through the door. He sheds his jacket, tossing it on the table in the foyer and jets toward the living room.

I would've been in trouble for that shit when I was his age. *Go hang that jacket up, young man.* I can hear my mom's voice plain as day. But nope, not Henry. The kid walks on water and heals the blind.

"Henry!" my mom calls out in excitement. "I've missed you!"

He laughs, colliding with her legs. "You saw me three days ago."

"Three days is too long," she says, squeezing him in a bear hug.

He squeals as she tickles his side. "Mom and Jude said Aunt Luce was leaving Penelope at home, but I told them that she wouldn't and that you wouldn't let her. Babies can't stay at home by themselves. Isn't that right, MeMe?"

My mother gives me *the look* over Henry's head. "That's right. Don't worry. Baby Penelope is in the kitchen with Pops."

"You never left Jude at home by himself when he was a baby, did you, MeMe?"

"Only once," she says, shrugging as she walks by. "But I came right back and got him."

What?

"That's right," Lucy says, chiming in on her way through the living room. "Mom left you in the car seat by the front door." My sister laughs like she's watching Comedy Central.

"That could've scarred me for life," I tell them.

"Oh, you were fine," my mother says, swatting me away. "You don't even remember. The only reason Lucy knows is because your father ratted me out."

"Don't let her fool you, son," my dad says, bouncing a small bundle in his arms as he walks slowly around the kitchen. "She was about to have a nervous breakdown when she called me and told me what happened."

My mother is now swatting him with the dishtowel on his ass, of course. I swear this is some sort of old people foreplay. Every time they start bantering in the kitchen and my mom swats him with a towel, he gets a look in his eyes. "You're over-exaggerating."

"Man with a baby here," my dad says, placing a protective hand on Penelope's little head.

"Oh, she's fine. Aren't you, beautiful," my mom coos to Penelope. "You like it when I spank Grandpa, don't you?"

"Hey! Let's keep it PG," Will says, walking into the kitchen. "We're not starting sex ed until she's at least old enough to talk."

"What's sex ed?" Henry asks.

"Nothing," we all sing in unison like a choir in church.

And everybody says amen.

"Seth W. says he hears his parents having sex," Henry says, settling in at the bar as my mom slides him a pre-dinner cookie. Something else that never would've happened when I was his age.

It's like hell hath frozen over and I didn't get the memo.

"Don't listen to Seth W.," my mom says.

"It's okay for parents to have sex. Right, Mom?" Henry asks.

Quinn rolls her eyes behind his back. "Yes, Henry."

"How old do you have to be before you have sex?"

"Really old," I tell him, rubbing up against Quinn. If the old people can do it, so can I.

"Do you and Pops have sex, MeMe?"

Why?

Why must Sunday dinners always end up in inappropriate conversations? You'd think having Henry and Penelope around would make things different, but nope. Just another generation of Harrises who are going to need therapy.

"You sure it's okay for Henry to stay the night?" I ask, helping Quinn with her jacket as we ease toward the door.

I'm only asking to be polite.

If she says no, I plan on throwing Quinn over my shoulder and making a run for it.

"He's already asleep. Besides, we love it when he stays the night. You know that."

"I know. Just making sure." I kiss her cheek and then lean my head out the door to push the remote start on Quinn's SUV. "Oh, and Daniel and Zach will be by to get him tomorrow morning. They're taking him to a Comic-Con thing."

"How fun!" my mom says, beaming.

She loves Daniel and Zach.

"I'll have to get up a little early and make them some banana nut muffins. Zach loves them. He brought my container back by last week and left the sweetest note and a bunch of flowers on the porch," she gushes, placing her hand over her heart. "*So sweet.*"

Yeah, so fucking sweet.

Daniel and Zach are becoming the friends you started to hate when you were little because your parents thought they were *so well-behaved* and that you should act more like them.

A few months ago, they bought my house. They're trying to adopt and needed a bigger place with a yard. Since Fergie and I were basically living at Quinn's anyway, I sold them my house. Now, they have coffee and cocktails with my parents on a regular basis. Will and Daniel golf on Saturdays. Zach has been helping my mom with her new website.

Somehow, we all fit.

It's weird, and it's unconventional and definitely not perfect. But it works.

Henry has three dads, kind of like that '90s television show, except there are three instead of two and we don't all live together. *Thank God*. He only refers to Daniel as dad, but that's okay with me. All I care about is that I get to be a part of his life. Everything's better with Quinn and Henry...a random Monday night, a random Tuesday night, Sundays at the park, Harris Family Dinners. All of it.

"Thanks again, Susan," Quinn says, leaning in for a hug.

After the door closes behind us, we can't get to the car fast enough.

"Drive fast," Quinn says, buckling her seat belt.

"Planned on it," I tell her, practically peeling out of the driveway. "We could stop in a back alley for a quickie."

"I want our bed."

Our bed.

Yeah, I want that too.

Five minutes later, we're pulling into the driveway. Before I even have the car in park, Quinn has her seatbelt off and the door halfway open.

We race each other up the sidewalk, and Quinn giggles as I struggle to get the door open.

"Stick it in, Harris. Geez," she teases, her hands sneaking under my shirt and down the waist of my jeans.

"Fuck," I groan, partially at the fucking lock that won't cooperate and partially at the fucking hot woman with her hands on me.

When I finally get it, I pull her in and press her up against the wall, kicking the door closed behind us. Blindly, I move us down the wall and press in the code for the alarm, disarming and then arming it again. Picking Quinn up in my arms, I walk quickly to the bedroom, my pants sagging because she's already managed to unbutton them and pull the zipper down.

She's fast.

As I toss her onto the bed, her hair fans out around her. She's so damn beautiful. And she's mine—made just for me.

"God, I love you," I tell her, pulling my shirt off and tossing it onto the floor.

"I love you, too," she says, ridding herself of her jeans and panties. No need for pretenses. We both know what's getting ready to go down here.

I brace my arms on either side of her, caging her in. "I'm gonna need this off too," I say, pulling at the edge of her shirt. "I want to see all of you."

Her face disappears from view for a second as she pulls the shirt over her head. I make quick work of her bra.

Thank you, Lord, for front clasps.

We take a second to let our eyes and hands roam, needing a minute to appreciate each other.

"Kiss me," she finally whispers.

I press my lips to hers and she opens her mouth, inviting me in. Her hands cup my jaw, but as the kiss intensifies, her fingers find my hair. I love when she's desperate and needy.

I love that she wants me as badly as I want her.

I love that we're always on the same page, whether it's fast and hard or slow and easy.

"I need to feel you inside me."

I love that she knows what she wants and she's not afraid to tell me.

I love that there are no longer any walls.

Just her.

And me.

I pull back and kneel in front of her, wanting to watch as I slide inside. Running my fingers between her slick heat, I groan. She's so wet, ready for me, always. "Fuck, Quinn. You feel so good."

Her hips lift up off the bed, forcing my fingers deeper. As she begins to ride my hand, I lean back and enjoy the show, my cock weeping, wanting to get in on the action.

"I'm gonna come," she says breathlessly, gripping the blanket beneath her. "Oh, God, I'm gonna come."

I press my thumb to her clit and continue to pump in and out of her. "You're so fucking beautiful," I tell her. "I love watching you come undone for me."

With a cry, her body tenses, and her walls tighten. Unable to wait another second, I hook my arms under her knees and pull her hips onto my lap, my cock slamming into her, causing her to cry out in pleasure. After a few hard thrusts, her body begins to tremble beneath me.

"Oh, my God," she chants, her hands moving from her sides to above her head as she comes back down from her high and joins in the game, pressing herself down. "Fuck."

Filthy words coming out of that beautiful mouth only makes me thrust harder and faster, leaning back to watch my cock slide in and out of her. In moments like these, when everything between us is raw and primal, I'm reminded of our beginning.

Then, everything about Quinn was a mystery. I didn't even know her name, but I knew her body called out to mine.

Now, I know everything about her—mind, body, and soul—and she is all I'll ever need.

When I look back up at her face, her eyes meet mine and she gives me that wicked smirk I love so much. "Don't look at me like that, Quinn. I swear to God. I'll lose my shit."

My words come out in quick bursts, drops of sweat beading up on my forehead.

"Go ahead," she taunts. "Do it. I want to see you come."

Growling, I tilt my head back and try to hang on as long as possible, willing myself to keep control, because this feels so damn good—*she* feels so damn good. I don't ever want to stop.

Quinn's moans and cries are what push me over the edge. Listening to her pleasure is what makes me come. My balls tighten, and then white light explodes behind my eyes. I swear, it's like I'm transformed into another dimension...some *Matrix* shit. I ride it out until my cock can't take it anymore. Quinn writhes beneath me, milking my orgasm.

When I'm spent and can no longer stay upright, I pull out of her and lie beside her, tucking her against me.

"I love you," I whisper, smoothing her hair.

"I love you," she replies, pressing her cheek against my chest.

Fucking Quinn is magnificent. But being with her like this is a close second.

Gone are the days of us meeting up in random hotel rooms.

Gone are the days of built-up walls and no strings attached.

We're all in.

Acknowledgements

Thank you for reading No Strings Attached! We're so happy to bring you Jude and Quinn's story. It's a little off-the-beaten-path for us but still has the same Jiffy Kate humor and heart. So, we hope you love it as much as we do.

As with all of our stories, we have a few people we'd like to thank.

First, we'd like to thank our crazy, awesome families. They give us inspiration and so much grace. We wouldn't be able to do what we do without them.

Second, we'd like to thank our team.

Pamela Stephenson, thank you for being an awesome alpha reader, sounding board, and cheerleader! We appreciate your presence in our lives and are so happy your YOU!

Nichole Strauss, thank you for being an amazing editor. Can you believe this is our twelfth book together? WOW. We appreciate you not kicking us to the curb and teaching us all the things along the way.

Juliana Cabrera, you knocked this cover OUT OF THE PARK!! Thank you for your creative insight and patience and for always working us in when we need you.

To our proofreader, Janice Owen, thank you for being so meticulous in your work.

And last, but certainly not least, we'd like to thank our super fun and supportive reader group, Jiffy Kate's Southern Belles. Y'all are the best! Thank you for always being there for us and reading our words. You're our favorite corner of the internet.

Much love,
Jiffy Kate

About The Authors

Jiffy Kate is the joint pen name for Jiff Simpson and Jenny Kate Altman. They're co-writing besties who share a brain. They also share a love of cute boys, good coffee, and a fun time.

Together, they've written over twenty stories. Their first published book, Finding Focus, was released in November 2015. Since then, they've continued to write what they know—southern settings full of swoony heroes and strong heroines.

You can find them on most social media outlets at @jiffykate, @jiffykatewrites, or @jiffsimpson and @jennykate77.

Made in the USA
Middletown, DE
12 May 2020

94126698R00106